As the Eagle Soars

At Birth and Beyond

As the Eagle Soars

At Birth and Beyond

Toni Tarango

ISBN: 979-8-9889721-1-2

Special Dedication

First and foremost, I want to acknowledge the efforts of Indigenous Elders and Culture Keepers throughout the North American continent. These individuals are the primary teachers within their communities. Elders and Culture Keepers are vital to the preservation of customs, knowledge, and traditions specific to the origins of their tribes. This is an enormously important and sacred task and one that I believe to be of extreme significance for both the Indigenous and non-Indigenous populations living on this planet.

As early as the 1830s, it was widely assumed that Native Americans were facing extermination. But the predictions were wrong. Entering the 20th century, Native American numbers began to rise. The upturn was gradual at first, but by 1990 the survival of Native North Americans was indisputable. This long, slow recovery to some seemed almost a fulfillment of the refrain in a century-old Comanche Ghost Dance song: "We shall live again; we shall live again" (*Through Indian Eyes: The Untold Story of Native American Peoples*, p. 353).

Today there are 574 federally recognized tribes in the USA, though there were likely to have been hundreds, if not thousands more throughout the history of the continent.

Preface

Around 2003, I took an introduction to fiction writing class at Berkeley City College in Berkeley, California. The framework for the original short story came from a personal conflict that occurred every time I filled out an employment application and was asked about "ethnicity and race." My father, Raul Flores Tarango (RIP 3/2019) was Mexican American and my mother, Sally Elaine Nave (RIP 1/2023) was of European descent. At that time, employment applications didn't have a "bicultural" box, and I often felt guilty checking the box for "Hispanic" or "Latino" because I didn't look the part. Plus, my last name was frequently thought to be of Italian origin, which didn't help matters. However, the job application dilemma got me thinking about how, at a deeper level, this might also be an issue for others, and that led to the extended version of this original short story. So, there you go: therein lies the genesis of this creation!

Decades ago, I had the privilege of working with Pima dialysis patients in a social services capacity. These individuals were members of the Gila River Indian Reservation aka Sacaton, located south of Chandler, AZ. I want to be clear that I do not claim to be an authority on Native American customs or traditions. The gatherings I describe in this story are based on what I recall from having attended similar functions decades ago and are not affiliated with the above-mentioned tribe. As the Eagle Soars – At Birth and Beyond is a work of fiction and in no way claims to document any custom or tradition with any degree of authority.

Toni Tarango
Author

Prologue

The voices of our ancestors, the Ancients, are well known to Native American elders. They echo within the geological structures of the Sonoran Desert. As the largest, hottest desert in North America, it will suck the life force out of any animal, plant, or human not prepared to handle the riveting heat. Such is the location of the town of Coleman and the nearby Nagchaw reservation of South- Central Arizona.

Living in the Sonoran Desert you become accustomed to planning your activities around the searing heat, especially during certain times of the year. This area experiences long, extremely hot summers and brief winters consisting of mild afternoons and chilly evenings. The area averages less than 10 inches of rain per year, which usually falls during the monsoon season from mid- June through late September.

In 1950, my father, Sam Gentry, a young man of Irish Catholic descent, left the Midwest and moved to Coleman and in 1960 founded Gentry Construction. For the last twenty plus years, his company has been the primary construction employer in the area. He invested deeply in the community by way of teaching construction basics and then hiring from Coleman and occasionally from the Nagchaw reservation.

My sister Joslin and I grew up in Coleman, which was founded in the early 1900's. Now 1980, the population is around 30,000. Coleman has the small-town basics: a small police department, a bank, library, post office, hospital, a grade, middle, and high school, St. Mary's Catholic Church, an LDS (Mormon) church. In addition, a Bashas' grocery store, a Bob's Big Boy, a Howard Johnson's, and the ever- popular Matta's Mexican restaurant. There is also a small Sears department store and a local Homestyle Bakery. Then, of course, there are a handful of gas stations and a couple of roughneck dive bars. Several of the Coleman businesses, like Bashas', Matta's, Sears, and Homestyle Bakery were built by Gentry Construction. This was greatly appreciated since the nearest shopping and dining options for Coleman residents were over 60 miles away in Tucson.

About ten miles outside of Coleman, running along the old meandering Snake River, is the Native American reservation known as Nagchaw with a population of 2,500. Established in 1858, Nagchaw was the home of my mother, Marta Yellowbird. The facilities on the reservation are far fewer than in Coleman. The Nagchaw Tribal Center houses the Tribal Council on the second floor and downstairs is our library and cultural center. Also on the reservation is a small grocery store, a gas station, and a break-fast-lunch spot, Naturally Native café, with the best Indian tacos this side of the Snake River. The largest onsite facility is the Native American Health Center which provides primary medical and dental care as well as outpatient drug and alcohol recovery services.

Chapter 1
Good Medicine

Medicine is essence, and essence is the most distinct and concentrated characteristic of a singular thing. Good medicine is the essence that's created when at least two things come together and create something good and positive.

Author: Doug Good Feather
from *Think Indigenous*

To this day, I still have an odd memory, or dream, or maybe a vision about my birth. It's hard to say what it was, exactly, but I remember certain things from that experience like it was yesterday. What I remember while looking up as I floated in a fluid source was seeing the world. What struck me about looking at the world was that I understood what this structure was about. As I was transfixed on the earth, I then saw a large brown eagle soaring above. Instinctively, I understood that the brown color of the eagle was the blending of raw ochre, sienna, and umber, which are the oldest pigments used in the prehistoric art of my mother's people, the Yellowbird clan of the Nagchaw Nation.

The Nagchaw believe Eagles represent great knowledge and transcendence. Eagles can rise above, which symbolizes the ability to observe life from a spiritually enlightened perspective, detached from simplistic ego desires. As symbols of freedom, Eagles are revered as fierce, powerful, and free.

That ability to connect and remember closed shortly after my birth, and it would be many years until I reconnected with this Ancient Source again.

On the day of my birth, it was hot, and the humidity was high from the monsoon season being in full swing. According to my mother Marta, my father, Sam Gentry, was away on a business trip in Phoenix and was not present at my birth. As my mother has always said, I was in a hurry and came earlier than expected. I'm told that my birth happened at home with a Nagchaw midwife, as my mother squatted over a bundle of soft blankets. I entered the world screaming at the top of my lungs.

My early childhood wasn't much different from most folks, I would imagine, except for growing up under the influence of two competing worldviews: the Indigenous and the Other, as I would come to call them.

Playing with children my age in the neighborhood was sprinkled with comments from their parents about "my color" or "my Indian-ness" as if it were something I could turn on and off. As a little boy, my mother allowed me to grow my hair longer than the other boys my age. By the age of 10, my appearance elicited teasing about being a sissy because the neighborhood boys thought I looked like a girl. My remedy for this conclusion was to prove to them that I was not a girl, which led to pushing, shoving, and rolling around in the dirt. These were not serious fights in my opinion because I most often found that these boys were not physically prepared to defend their opinions.

"Keith, what have I told you about fighting with those boys? You know that they and their parents think that we're just a bunch of uncivilized Indians." Mom said, looking distraught as she noticed my hands curled into fists.

"Ma, I don't care what they think, or their stupid parents. Being Native American is way better than being an ignorant fool and looking like milk toast, don't you think?" I huffed.

These kinds of tussles were sprinkled throughout late grade school and middle school, but the summer before my freshman year saw four inches of growth. By high school these altercations ceased as I focused on developing my athletic skills. I was just shy of 6' and a wide receiver, but football was my second love. Where I felt most at home was on the Coleman High track team, which highlighted my ability to run like the wind. Yes, I was much faster than all those other boys, and I knew that it irked a couple of the more popular ones.

By high school my hair hung well below my shoulders and my coaches urged me to cut it. I refused, stating that if it made a difference in my ability, only then would I agree to cut it.

"Coach, you know short hair is a white man's thing, right? Long hair in our culture is a guy thing. Plus, look at all the great warriors throughout history, they all had long hair." I said.

"What are you talking about? What warriors, besides Indians, had long hair? Educate me Gentry." Coach said.

"Okay, there's this book in the library, it has drawings of long hair being worn by all the warriors. Yeah, way back to the Greeks, the Vikings, and the Samurai, they all had long hair. Plus, the Samurai considered long hair a symbol of honor. If they screwed up and did something dishonorable, then they'd cut their hair. I swear Coach, check out the book Ancient Warriors in the library." I said.

"Well, I just might do that. So, Gentry, are you writing a paper on ancient warriors? Still, I think that short hair looks better, a much more clean-cut look, but I won't discourage you wearing long hair since it's been said that it's a cultural thing." Coach said as he laughed slightly.

Coleman High had a dress code which didn't allow long hair on boys except for those of us who were Native American. Yes, there had been a big parent-teacher battle at a monthly PTA meeting. A dozen Nagchaw parents protested that their sons were being forced to dishonor their heritage by wearing "white boy haircuts." That viewpoint did not go over well with many in Coleman, still, those of us who excelled at sports were allowed to wear our hair long without being hassled.

The older I got, the more I was aware of a deep resentment that lay just below the surface of my disarming personality. In high school I wasn't secure enough to fully buck the system. Yet, when the opportunity presented itself, I challenged established viewpoints on several things. Even if the challenge wasn't successful, doing so got my point across. This resulted in my getting a reputation for being a sort of student advocate, which put me in favor with the popular kids.

Although it was rarely spoken about, a few years earlier, the Occupation of Alcatraz from the fall of 1969 to the summer of 1971 had greatly affected those of us with Nagchaw roots. That 19-month-long protest by 89 Native Americans included two individuals from the reservation, or "Rez" as we called it. These individuals were held in great esteem by the Nagchaw population, including my mother. Although I was only a kid at the time, I intuitively felt the importance of that situation. I entered my teen years proud of my heritage and not willing to cower to anyone who saw me as inferior, not even my father.

My father, on the other hand, was very outspoken about how awful he thought those "damn Indians" were who organized the Alcatraz Occupation. He always stated, within earshot, that if I or my kid sister Joslin ever participated in anything like that, we'd be disowned by him forever.

Sam Gentry was not an easy man to love. Yes, as my father, I do recall a few happy memories playing catch with him as a little boy, although I greatly disappointed him when I didn't go out for the Coleman High baseball team. I tried explaining that track and football were my favorite team sports, and baseball was my least favorite. That, unfortunately, was viewed as a grave error in judgement from my father's perspective.

Unfortunately, sports were only one area where he and I were often at odds. Sam believed that I was "too Indian," as he used to say. He had little, if any, respect for the Nagchaw culture and traditions, and this was a major point of contention between us. And, to top it all off, I looked like my mother as far as my warm brown complexion, long chestnut brown hair, and green eyes. His viewpoint created a deep wound between us since I knew he felt that my appearance would be a major handicap throughout my lifetime.

So much value is put on one's physical appearance. Although I look like my mother's people, the Nagchaw, my younger sister does not.

Joslin with her fair complexion, amber eyes, and auburn hair displays the Gentry genes through and through. If you were to listen to my father talk about that, you'd swear he thought I was somebody else's son.

As a kid there are plenty of things about your parents that you don't fully understand, but you know when something you've done is not appreciated and seen as unacceptable behavior. My father would take off his leather belt and hold it while speaking to me about something he wasn't in agreement with. My mother would always speak up and tell him that there is a better way to make his point, but he rarely if ever listened to his wife about those kinds of things.

My mother never spoke to my dad about the tussles I had with the neighborhood boys growing up. She always said, "It's best that your dad does not know about some things," and needing to defend myself surely wasn't anything he wanted to hear about.

I'll never forget when I was in the sixth grade and got sent to the principal's office for fighting. The school called home but apparently my mother was out, so they called my father at work. Sam was not one bit happy about that and even less so when he found out I gave one of his workers' kids a black eye. When he got to the school he was fuming.

"What in God's name do you think you're doing Keith? Have you lost your mind or were you just proving a point that you're a damn Indian and can act like one too?" Sam said with disdain.

It was then, at that exact moment, that I clearly understood that Sam, like many others, saw me as less important and not worth defending. In my heart of hearts, I knew this viewpoint to be wrong, but when you're dealing with your father and an entire population who sees something differently than you, it's not easy to speak up.

After the meeting with the Principal, Sam dropped me off at home. Before I opened the front door, I looked down and saw a pair of worn, brown leather shoes sitting by the entrance. These shoes were distinct and unlike anything you could buy in a department store. These were the shoes worn by my mother's father, who we called Pawpaw. Pawpaw rarely came to our home as he didn't like being around Sam. Most often our mom would take us to the Rez, and we'd visit Pawpaw and Grandma Moon there.

Pawpaw was the positive male figure in my life. He took time to share his thoughts and feelings with me about life, about being Native American. He said I was gifted with the heart and soul of our Nagchaw ancestors, the Ancients.

"Grandson, I got a feeling that you needed to see me today, so here I am. Why are you home from school so early? Is everything okay at school? Are they treating you with respect?" Pawpaw said with an expression on his face that made me think he already knew what was going on.

Pawpaw was funny like that. This wasn't the first or the last time that he would show up to check on me. He always seemed to show up at a point when I really needed a strong male influence that was of a positive nature

"I got sent home for fighting. A kid in my class called me a 'Slimy Indian' and said that I smelled like the rear end of a dog. I thought it was funny that he claimed to know what a dog's rear end smelled like and pointed that out. It got everyone laughing and that's when he took a swing at me. I swung back and gave him a black eye, which got me sent to the principal's office, where they called Dad." I said looking down at the floor.

"Aww yes, it's odd how the White's know so much about that smell. Perhaps if they were less full of it themselves, they wouldn't smell it everywhere they go." Pawpaw said with a big grin on his face. Pawpaw had a real sense of humor, which was in great supply whenever he was talking about the Others, as he and I called the non-Indigenous folks.

Pawpaw was deeply connected to the Ancestors. He would stress that during our short time on Mother Earth we either repeat old patterns and ways of viewing or we open the door to something new. He would tell me that once I was able to hear and feel what a person held in their heart, I would recognize which ones were of like mind. He would tell me that humans are not separate from nature but are nature itself. We are all connected, a part of the whole and not separate from it. Pawpaw was the wisest person I knew, and I was grateful to have him in my life.

Chapter 2
Two Sides One Coin

The creator—Great Spirit—is the awareness that allows both the existence of... and the possibility and potential of every-single-thing. As the physical form of a spiritual being, each of us is a fully realized manifestation of the Creator that we chose to co-create. And our purpose in life is to express our self as the highest and best version of this life that we chose.

Author: Doug Good
Feather from *Think Indigenous*

Only as an adult did I come to understand the importance of transparency. Having grown up in a household where the primary male figure disrespects not only you, but your mother, you will do one of two things. You'll either model your father's attitudes and behavior, or you will strike out against anyone that remotely resembles those attitudes and behaviors including the person who introduced them to you. There were so many times that I wanted to physically confront Sam, but knowing that would greatly disturb my mother, I never did. She would often tell me that as a young man he had been very different. Her insistence led me to wonder what had happened that caused him to change to the way he is now, cold hearted, small minded, and a Nagchaw- hater.

As I found refuge in team sports, I was able to focus less on Sam and his deprived ways and more on what I believed would be my reality—a reality that I could choose and decide how and what I wanted to be. As I excelled in both football and track, I found that I was being scouted by four educational institutions: Arizona State, the University of Arizona, New Mexico State, and the University of New Mexico. Although I was the number two Coleman High prospect, I was an honor roll student and that seemed to appeal to the scouts.

Coleman High's number one athlete, a defensive lineman, Jack Mitchell was at best, a D+ student. Oh, now, they were still watching and talking to Jack and his parents, but the caveat was that Jack had to get better grades. It seems that colleges and universities were less inclined to give full ride scholarships to athletes who couldn't graduate from a liberal arts program. Anyone who knew Jack Mitchell knew he was hard pressed to spell the word "liberal."

He also reminded me of my father as far as his attitude about Nagchaw went. Oh, he was cordial, but I would often catch him staring at me in the courtyard during lunch and I wondered what he was thinking. From the look on his face, whatever it was, I knew it wasn't something I wanted to hear. Jack never really spoke much to me. When he did say anything remotely related to me or my athletic abilities, it was always a derogatory comment about being a second-rate athlete because I was Nagchaw. I would usually smirk at him and say something to the effect of: "Yeah Jack, only in your dreams are you close to being as good of an athlete as I am. Oh yeah, and a good student too." Usually that was enough to shut him up, but the look in his eyes told me that at some point there'd be a physical confrontation. Coach Tompkins stressed that there would be no fighting in school among his team members. If there was, both would be suspended the first time. The second time, both would find themselves off the team for good.

It was a Friday afternoon during last period when Jack came up to me. I was putting my books away before heading to the locker room to change and go out on the field for practice. Jack slammed my locker shut and kept his hand on the door.

"You think you're so damn smart, don't you Gentry. Well, I know better, cause you ain't nothin' but an ignorant Indian," Jack said.

"So, you've decided to get suspended? *Ayuu nyoysh mknaamuum* [a warning against bad behavior]," Keith said.

"What? What did you call me? What does that mean? You ain't supposed to use no devil's language at school. That'll get you expelled for good you know," Jack said.

Right at that moment, Coach Tompkins came around the corner. Seeing the intensity between us he immediately called out to Jack:

"Don't go there, Jack! You know whatever you're beefing about isn't worth being suspended. Now, what's going on?"

"Naw, Coach, nothing's going on. I was just asking Gentry when our next math test was gonna be, Jack said.

"Oh yeah? "Humm, you know Jack, you need to get your grades up and I think that's a great idea! Yes, I think Keith would make an excellent tutor," Coach said.

"Wait, wait Coach...that's not what we were talking about."

"No way coach, I didn't say anything like that! I ain't letting no ignorant Indian teach me nothing!" Jack huffed.

"You might want to rethink that, Jack. This so-called ignorant Indian has a 3.7 GPA, which is an A minus," Coach said. "Well, if you two don't work out whatever you're beefing about, I'll have you paired for tutoring, plain and simple. So, you'd better work out whatever is going on or you'll be seeing each other an additional three times a week for an hour. God knows you need it, Jack!" Coach said as he winked at me and walked into the teacher's lounge.

Coach Tompkins was well-known for nipping conflicts in the bud, so to speak. He was aware of what the beef was as he'd spoken to me about it already. Coach encouraged me not to take anything Jack said personally, or feed into anything he did that seemed to be directed at me. He stated that Jack found me threatening. Coach was determined to use that to motivate Jack toward self-improvement, however, his plan may have backfired. It now seemed that Jack resented me even more than he previously had.

Little did I understand then that Jack's attitude toward me was really a reflection of his own self-loathing. Jack almost didn't graduate from Coleman High, and he never got that athletic scholarship because of his poor grades. He ended up working for my dad as a laborer at Gentry Construction and never amounted to much. I see him from time to time coming out of The 5th Amendment, a seedy little bar on the outskirts of town.

His anger seems to have been replaced by a sense of having been defeated. It's sad really, and I've wondered who in his life supported that self-fulfilling prophecy.

I wondered about things like that with my sister Joslin, too. She's five years younger, and very different. She'd much rather stay at home on the weekend and read a book or work on her art. She's very creative, especially when it comes to using several kinds of materials. It doesn't matter if it's shells, stones, beads, buttons, cloth, felt, yarn, leather, or paint. You name it, and Joslin can create something beautiful with any material. To top it all off, she's the real academic of the family and had been moved up a grade in elementary school and again in middle school. In high school I had to study to maintain my 3.7 GPA— but not Joslin. She rarely studied and her GPA was the same as mine. Now, tell me, how fair is that?

Her experience with being bicultural is also very different than mine. She often seems guilty about having Indigenous roots. When I've asked her what's up with that, she speaks about feeling like a fraud because she doesn't look the part. I reminded her more than once that 50%, gives her a legitimate right to call herself a Native American, but somehow that's an issue for her. It's true, she looks more like Sam than our mother, but it's what's in the blood that counts, and I've told her that over and over.

When we walk to the Snake River in the early evenings, I've made a sincere effort to talk with her about how it is that I feel connected to the Nagchaw, and especially to the Yellowbird clan, our mother's people. I've also shared with her my experiences of the medicine circles and sweats I've gone to. She always seems interested, and she asks good questions, but I don't think she sees these traditions or ceremonies as having meaning for her. I've spoken to our mother about that, and she agrees that Joslin struggles with feeling connected to her Indigenous roots. Our mother had tried to find a way for Joslin to become involved with community projects on the Rez. Being a part of a project and having a role would most likely help her feel like a part of the tribe, Mom had hoped.

A while back, while visiting Pawpaw and Grandma Moon, she said something to me about Joslin. Grandma Moon has always seemed to have a special place in her heart for Joslin. Grandma said that one day Joslin would come to know and understand her Medicine. Now, that was a powerful statement. I didn't ask any questions, but I understood that meant her time is coming. And, when that time comes, her sense of being connected will come to life. She will, I hope, be open to a new understanding of herself and her life's purpose. As odd as this sounds, I've dreamt about her future, as well as mine. In my dreams, I'm the initiator and Joslin is the fulfillment of the Ancestors voices. I have plans for my future and the tribe's and I would be honored to have my sister alongside me in bringing about change to the Nagchaw. Often, these dreams are kind of fuzzy and out of focus, but their message is clear.

Change is never an easy thing, I have found. Fifteen years earlier, at almost 20, before I decided to leave my childhood home, I went up north into the forest outside of Sedona. It was a strange four days: I took very few provisions and I managed to live off the land during this time. I remember feeling something churning from deep within. I knew it was about my future, who I was, and what my life would become. I was in that place Pawpaw sometimes spoke about and called "the place between dreams." I went about those four days in silence, backpacking, fishing, cooking, sleeping out under the stars in a headspace that was an empty nameless place. That was a place between what had been and what would come to pass. In this empty nameless place, I was aware of a constant internal churning. It felt as if something were about to spring forth into existence, but what that was exactly, I wasn't sure. I just knew that living at home, in Sam's house, no longer seemed to fit me. It was like trying to fit into an old pair of jeans that I had outgrown but was still trying to wear.

When I returned from this venture, I knew that the time had come. I was going to leave my childhood home and move elsewhere, most likely onto the Rez. I went to see my then best buddy, Mike Milton. Mike, now in his 40's, was single back then, and he too loved backpacking, fishing, and living off the land. He grew up on the Rez and went through school in Coleman and then onto the University of Arizona in Tucson.

Mike worked at a drug and alcohol outpatient program in Tucson, but after a couple of years he quit. He said he saw the need for something like this on the Rez, but he felt that this program wouldn't mesh well with the Nagchaw culture. After leaving, he got involved with the Tribal Council and convinced them that an outpatient drug and alcohol program attached to the primary care clinic was a logical fit and urgently needed, and they bought it. Then he convinced the Native American Health Center's Medical Director, Doc Watson, that such a program was essential for the wellbeing of the Nagchaw tribe. Within a few months, he lobbied the Bureau of Indian Affairs for funds, applied for a grant, and opened the rehab program and is now running it. Anyway, Mike understood the churning I spoke about and said that he too had spent some time in that "place between dreams." He said that when you honor that call to be alone, Great Spirit knows you are ready and up for any task that you might be called to take on. And that's exactly what happened. Mike went on to design, plan, and execute an outpatient program which incorporated indigenous values and traditions. The Thunder Road Recovery Program focuses on clean and sober living, right livelihood, and is what it is today because of Mike Milton's ability to hear the Ancestors and listen to Great Spirit.

Chapter 3

Waiting in the Wings of Your Life

Whether you chose your change or not, there are unlived potentialities within you, interests and talents, that you have not yet explored. Transitions clear the ground for new growth.

Author: William Bridges, from *Transitions*

I had been on the verge of leaving Sam's house in Coleman for a while now. At just about twenty, I thought I was a grown man. Compared to many of the kids I went to school with, I probably was. There had been a certain kind of questioning happening about life since I was a kid. That whole process of questioning revolved around figuring out where I fit in outside of my family and who my people were. When I first moved out, I lived in an old sandwich house on the Rez for a few months which had been updated with electricity and running water. The sandwich house walls were layered with wooden planks, cardboard, and corrugated tin, and often these primitive structures did not have running water or electricity.

Then my good buddy, Mike Milton, who also lived on the Rez in a two-bedroom townhouse, asked me if I wanted to move in. Mike was an ambitious guy who was tackling graduate school in Tucson at the University of Arizona. When taking classes three days a week, Mike stayed at his cousin's house. Then, on Thursday morning Mike would drive back to Nagchaw until he had to leave for Tucson again on Monday. He preferred not to leave his place unoccupied while in Tucson, and he knew I'd been living in an old sandwich house. His place was close to the center of the Rez, and the spare room was already furnished. All I needed to bring were my clothes and personal items. There was also a shed outside next to the carport where I could store my bike and other items.

Although Mike was six years older than I was, we had a connection. He was the only friend I had where we could sit in complete silence or talk for hours about all kinds of off-the- reservation things of a social, political, and environmental nature. And yes, women too. We had lively conversations without either of us getting bent out of shape if the other one didn't completely agree. Having grown up with Sam Gentry, I wasn't used to that kind of unconditional acceptance. I appreciated that Mike was a deep thinker who seemed to be able to look at two sides of a situation or idea without being overly attached to his original opinion. He also had a great sense of humor, which made him very entertaining to be around.

The morning I decided to tell my parents that I wanted to move out created some anxiety. Still, it was something that I knew I had to do. My backpacking venture to the woods above Sedona helped clarify why I had been in "the place between dreams" and what my next step would be.

"Mom, Dad, I know this might seem sudden to you both, but I've been wrestling with this idea for a while now. I want to move out and live on the Rez. Thompson's old sandwich house has got electricity and running water now, and it's sat empty since they left for Flagstaff. Mr. T. said I could live there as long as I wanted, and the rent is very reasonable."

The silence was thick, and I got nervous waiting for a response. It must have taken at least a couple of minutes before either of them said anything. I could see just a glint of approval in Mom's eyes, but Sam, well he just looked shocked.

"Keith, you know I'd rather have you here, but I understand that the time has come for you to leave the nest. I've sensed that a change was coming, but I hoped that it wouldn't involve you moving out. Still, I know the Thompson's and I think their little updated house suits you well. And I love that you'll be close to my family. I know Pawpaw will be especially happy about that," Mom said as she glanced at Sam.

"Let me get this straight. You want to leave your home, here, where you have everything you need and don't pay rent, so that you can go live on that hell hole of a reservation and pay rent?" Sam said as he walked to the liquor cabinet and poured himself a bourbon.

"Look dad, I know you don't see anything of value on the Rez or what happens there, but I do. I know I can't change your mind about that, so I won't even try. You know, I'm looking forward to living near the Yellowbird side of the family, finally," I said.

"It figures you'd choose to move there and relate to that bunch rather than stay here and eventually manage and run Gentry Construction. Keith, I know that you'd be a good foreman and eventually a great contractor. I don't understand why you're so hot to be a part of the reservation. What damn good will that do you, huh? When I first met your mother, I thought those people were kind of interesting, but as time passed, I saw that they were only interested in their next drink. Yeah, I know, I drink too, but at least I can control it," Sam said sheepishly, looking down at the floor.

"Look Dad, I'll be honest with you. Aside from the labor work you paid me to do during school breaks, I have tried to see myself working in your business, but it just doesn't appeal to me. It lacks something that I can't put my finger on at this moment. Yes, it would be a secure and reliable income given how this area has started to grow, but Dad, it's just not for me," I said.

"Alright, go on, get the hell out. I'm sure you'll enjoy gettin' your swerve on in animal skins with feathers glued to your ass as you juke to a drumbeat," Sam said angrily as he slammed his glass on the bar and left the room. A few minutes later we heard the back screen door slam shut. He revved his truck engine as he backed out of the driveway and sped off.

In anger, with his last statement, Sam slammed powwows. Sam had always refused to go with us when powwow time rolled around. Growing up, our mother took me and my sister to three Intertribal powwows a year, and that tradition continued as we became adults. During the summers, we went to one in Sedona and one in Flagstaff, and we went every October to the third one in Tucson. As our mother had shared with us, a powwow is a celebration where people from diverse indigenous nations gather for the purpose of drumming, dancing, singing, and honoring the traditions of their ancestors. Sam's disrespect for the traditions and ceremonies of the Nagchaw deeply bothered me. He was my father, and often I felt like he was a black hole at the center of my life, and that bothered me too. I felt lucky to have Pawpaw and my buddy Mike Milton in my life. These were men I looked up to, like I should have been able to do with my father but could not.

When the Powwow dancers make their Grand Entrance in their regalia, it is something to behold. Their most cherished regalia are carefully chosen and constructed of woven cloth or buckskin and might include a bandolier or a bone breastplate and flowing feather attachments. The jewelry, the colorful garments, and wide range of accessories are all striking. Some dancers might wear a traditional ribbon shirt or a vest, and many wear eagle feathers which are sacred symbols of Mother Earth and represent the unity of all things.

Powwows are celebrations, social gatherings where Mom, Jos, and I would catch up with old friends. And sometimes we'd make new friends from other tribes. There are also food booths where we'd get delicious Indian tacos made with fry bread, green chili cornbread, as well as traditional dishes for those times when hot dogs and hamburgers weren't satisfying enough. For many who lived on the reservation, the traditional dishes were a treat as those were only made for special occasions. Yes, homemade chili or a bowl of wild rice or red beans, with a mixture of potatoes, corn, and squash with beef, pork, or venison added was something many looked forward to. Then there were the craft tables where original works of art are sold like dream catchers, blankets, pottery, beadwork, leather work, and silver and turquoise jewelry. As you might expect, my artistically inclined sister loved scouring the craft tables at the powwows. Eventually, Joslin also had a craft table which displayed her creative talents and did well at the powwows.

One year in Flagstaff, Joslin found a jewelry table and spent over a half an hour debating between three beautiful, handmade silver rings. Her final selection had a moonstone at the center of a flower design, which she wears to this day. I have never seen her without that ring or her three silver twist bracelets. Her silver twist bracelets were gifts from me on her 16th, 18th, and 21st birthdays.

At the same Powwow where Joslin found her ring, I met someone who would become an important person in my life, Telrica Tusoni. She was 5'9" and a knockout. Her warm brown complexion, sparkling brown eyes, and long black hair were captivating. When Telrica walked into a room, you automatically felt as though someone important had entered. She was always delighted to embrace any such impressions you might imagine of her having serious social clout or status. I found her to be vivacious, theatrical, and passionate. Yes, she loved basking in the spotlight and always managed to be the center of attention. Her playful reputation meant that she enjoyed cultivating anything that was artistically and creatively inspired. Her reputation also reflected that she had a knack for attracting drama- fueled romances. Because her romances were known to cause an uproar with the more conservative crowd on the reservation, she now lives in Coleman. Telrica was perceived by her Nez clan as a diva who never tired of fancy dinners, parties, or expensive designer clothes, which were hard to come by in Coleman. When it was all said and done, she loved to dazzle those she associated with, which included me. I found Telrica to be full of life and vitality. She was a fearless optimist who refused to accept failure, and this was, in part, what drew me to her. We both were known for our ambition and determination, which was at the heart of the mutual attraction.

"So, are you just going to gawk at me or come over here and say something?" Telrica said as she stood in line for fry bread.

"Hey now, you jumped the gun. I was just about to come and get in line behind you and say *A'ho*!" I said, blushing as we both laughed.

"I know who you are. You're that Apple whose dad owns the construction company in town," Telrica said.

"Wow...Apple...no one's ever called me an Apple. I guess there's a first time for everything," I said, slightly annoyed.

"Well, aren't you an Apple? Red on the outside and white on the inside?" Telrica slyly asked.

"You might want to be careful when making assumptions about folks who are mixed, you know. I may have grown up with a white father, but my mother is Marta Yellowbird, and she would take offence to you calling me an Apple," I said grimacing.

"Oh, I've heard of Marta Yellowbird and Grandma Moon. Your grandma's a healer and she can see the future through her dreams and visions. Yes, I was brought up hearing about the Nagchaw side of your family. She's a powerful medicine woman, your grandma. I'd love to meet her and see what's up with my future," Telrica said on a more serious note. "Well, I might be able to arrange that, if you play your cards right," I said grinning.

Over the next 3-4 hours, we made the rounds talking with old friends and several dancers. Then we hit the craft and food booths. I found it amusing that this woman had no qualms about sampling the variety of delicious dishes being offered. Her lust for life seemed to go hand in hand with a healthy appetite.

"So, are you here with anyone other than your family?" I asked.

"Nope, I came with my parents, auntie, and a couple of cousins. We'll be heading back soon, before the closing, unless I can find another way home."

"I drove my mother and sister here and I'll introduce you when we run into them. You're welcome to ride back with us if you'd like. We never leave before the closing ceremony has ended."

"Okay, great, that works for me! Let me find my cousin and let her know I'm gonna stay and ride back with you," Telrica said as she took off toward the parking lot.

Before she returned, I found my mother and sister. I let them know that my friend wanted to stay until the closing ceremony, but her family was leaving early, so I had offered her a ride back to Coleman.

"Sure Keith, we always have enough room in the Suburban for an extra friend or two. We'll be leaving right after the closing ceremony, so please make sure she knows this," Mom said. After meeting my mother and Joslin, Telrica and I spent the rest of the Powwow together, talking, laughing, and getting a feel for what each other was about. As freewheeling as Telrica presented herself to be, I sensed a seriousness about her as it related to living a life beyond the frivolous, which is what she was known for.

Chapter 4
Walking the Path Together Barefoot

In this place we call time and space to what degree do we really see the path we walk or why it is we've come to talk. Could it be that familiar sense is really no pretense but perhaps a treasure map of times forgotten but not lost. At any rate, Spirit now brings us face to face in relationship that's not about time or space.

Prose By: Toni Tarango, 1997

Over the next few months, Telrica and I spent a lot of time together on the reservation with Pawpaw, Grandma Moon, and other Yellowbird family members. Later in the year, we attended the Tucson powwow, and then a sweat, along with a couple of medicine circles which Grandma Moon led. Telrica met privately with Grandma for a consultation about her future. Telrica was intent on knowing how her intentions might best be aligned with Mother Earth. This included drinking Grandma Moon's ritually prepared herbal tea each morning. Grandma believed strongly that it is important to have a compatible physical resonance with Mother Earth. When aligning our human intentions with that which grows from her soil, a tangible connection is created.

"Keith, do you see yourself living anywhere else besides the reservation?" Telrica asked.

"No, not really. Why?"

"I just wondered if you ever dream about how your life could be, in another place, doing something else.".

"What? Yes, of course I do, but not elsewhere. My dream is here. I dream of so many things that could be better for my family and others on this reservation. My dream includes one day being involved with the Tribal Council and helping the Nagchaw come into more modern times without giving up our traditions, and values," I said.

"It sounds like we have very different dreams. Of course, those dreams will probably lead to very different futures." Telrica's face revealed a sadness that she could not hide.

"Keith, I don't see my future here, in the Arizona desert," she continued. "I want to go to Hollywood and act like Tantoo Cardinal, Graham Green, Wes Studi, Rodney A. Grant, and the others. I know I can do what they've done as well, if given a chance. I'm an actress at my core and Hollywood is where I want to be," Telrica said.

"Yes, I can see you acting in Hollywood, but not at this point. Maybe you should try taking some smaller steps, here, closer to home. I've heard that there is a theater group or something like that in Tucson, so why not get involved with them first. That could be what opens a few doors for you, that and your dazzling personality," I laughed.

"Okay, my brilliant man, that's an excellent idea, but guess what? I've already reached out to the 'Tucson Theater Company,' and I'll be trying out for a part in an upcoming play in the next few weeks! The director said he'd like me to try out for the lead female role, and I jumped at the chance. Just think Keith, I'll be the star of the play!" Telrica said with glee.

This conversation embodied what I had always felt about my beautiful, sultry lover. In my heart, I always felt that her time here in the Arizona desert was limited. I knew but didn't want to admit that at some point she would take off for higher ground to follow her life's calling. She was destined for a different kind of greatness is what my heart told me early on. Still, it didn't stop me from embarking on the ride of my life as far as having an intimate relationship with her. She was and will always be the love of my life.

The next couple of years went by quickly as we continued seeing each other while developing our separate interests. I clearly felt that our combined realities were multilayered. In my heart of hearts, I knew that our different realities would eventually make themselves known. We moved in unison with joy and without thinking about what the inevitable redirection of our relationship would be. I had not mentioned anything about Telrica's desire to leave and move to Hollywood to my family. It was simply better if we kept what we both knew between us for now. Knowing that our time together was limited made the everyday activities like riding to or from Coleman or Nagchaw, or trips to Bashas' for groceries, or out to dinner at our favorite Matta's Mexican Restaurant very special. On a deeper level we both understood that supporting one another in fulfilling our destinies was vital to becoming who we were meant to be.

Chapter 5

Honoring the Ground We Stand On

The soil was soothing, strengthening, cleansing, and healing. This is why the old Indian still sits upon the earth instead of propping himself up and away from its life-giving forces. To sit or lie upon the ground is to be able to think more deeply and feel more keenly; he can see more clearly into the mysteries of life and come closer in kinship to others about.

-- Chief Luther Standing Bear

After graduating from Arizona State University with a bachelor's degree in business administration, I interviewed and was offered a full-time job at a Nonprofit organization called Terros, Inc. in Phoenix. The position was as their business manager, and it was a flattering offer which I seriously pondered and then turned down. During school I had worked at one of their residential treatment centers in Tempe. It was that experience that helped me decide that I wanted to bring these kinds of services to Nagchaw only with a culture-specific focus. My buddy, Mike Milton, had followed almost the same path only at a Tucson program when he decided to pursue that option via a Bureau of Indian Affairs grant for Nagchaw. Now, his program was an established department of the Native American Health Center. Part-time, I was running a support group for those in Mike's program. Although I had a drug and alcohol certificate, my real desire was to get more involved with the decision making that was happening within the walls of the Nagchaw Tribal Council.

Mike and I had spent hours talking about the need for the revitalization of the reservation and what services and programs would be most beneficial to those living on Nagchaw. I believe that Mike and I were both viewed as "progressives," and that wasn't necessarily a compliment within the somewhat conservative tribal council. That being said, we did have one sympathetic council member who felt that our ideas were very much needed and on point for Nagchaw. This council member would prove to be an important intermediary when it came to addressing issues and introducing new and updated systems and methods of management for the judicial administration of Tribal government. Lucy Keeton, a 58-year-old lifelong resident and dear friend of Grandma Moon, would prove to be invaluable as Mike and I moved toward addressing the needs of the tribe with solutions outside of traditional methods.

Lucy was one of four women who occupied the twelve Tribal Council seats. She had run the little Nagchaw elementary school before parents started sending their children into Coleman. Lucy had expressed a fear that was coming to fruition. Her fear revolved around the loss of identity by folks as it related to the traditions of the Nagchaw culture. Lucy spoke to both Mike and me separately, and then together, about what she saw happening. Lucy felt that the outside world was creeping onto the reservation by way of our young people's exposure to the outside. Mike, on the other hand, was dealing with the same longstanding issue as the need for drug and alcohol recovery services continued to surge. It was a long-standing yet worthwhile battle dealing with the generational effects of alcohol abuse. Children in families with one or both parents who were addicted to alcohol were significantly more likely to become alcoholics themselves. Making resources available and collaborating with the Tribal Council to address and provide recovery options was a challenge. Mike's program, Thunder Road Recovery, was training paraprofessionals to be outreach workers on the reservation. Each outreach worker had successfully completed the drug and alcohol certificate program and most of them were living on the reservation.

The traditional views of the Tribal Council often got in the way of progress, and it was a challenge that both Mike and I were willing to take on. We knew we had the support and backing of Lucy Keeton, and she, Mike, and I met with the Council of Elders on the reservation. The Council of Elders was an informal but significantly influential group on the reservation.

Pawpaw was on the council as was Grandma Moon, and both were in favor of doing whatever was necessary to bring healing and wholeness to the Nagchaw Nation, knowing that the effects would resonate for the next seven generations.

Starting with a health and wellness focus was important as that was directly connected to the next steps toward economic revival. The Tribal Council was tossing around ideas about bringing revenue-generating projects onto the reservation. Bringing essential goods and services that would support the well-being of the tribe was the area that I felt I could be of assistance. Interest had been expressed by a handful of tribal members in owning and operating small businesses. Understanding the advantage of developing an entrepreneurial spirit on Nagchaw would be a win-win for all. The Council of Elders in their wisdom understood the importance of rooting the wellness programs and services within the tribe before bringing the economic development projects onboard. These changes would allow the tribe to be rooted in health and wholeness so that a successful transition could take place leading to economic development. The next step was to start working with the Tribal Council to calm their fears about making so many significant changes. The Nagchaw Nation had survived without this kind of change for a long time. There had been more than one Chief Executive and a handful of seated members over the years who had used their offices for their personal financial gain. That, as I saw it, was at the root of the fears lying just below the surface of the resistance of more than half of the council members. Fortunately, that stance was not held by the Chief Executive who had expressed favor with many of our views and ideas.

Around this time, a council member had taken ill, and per the recommendation of his physician, he would take leave from his duties temporarily. The Tribal Council had asked Mike Milton to fill in, but he respectfully declined stating he was too busy. The council then asked Mike to recommend someone to fill in since he was unable to. The timing couldn't have been any better, which was how I got my foot in the door as a council stand-in. I was given an opportunity to quell the fears of those on the Tribal Council who thought of me as merely the son of Sam Gentry. Sam had a reputation on the reservation for being anti-Nagchaw, and most believed him to be a heartless human being. I completely understood that perception and believed that I would need to earn the trust of the council as far as being a true advocate for the Nagchaw Nation.

Chapter 6

The Nature of Power

You only are as powerful as that for which you stand. Do you stand for the beauty and compassion of each soul? Do you stand for forgiveness and humbleness? These are the stands of the personality that has aligned itself with its soul. This is the position of a truly powerful personality. Power is energy that is formed by the intentions of the soul.

Author: Gary Zukav, from *Seat of the Soul*

The Nagchaw Nation, like all tribes, have the power to govern themselves. Each federally recognized tribe retains the rights of an independent sovereign nation apart from the local, state, or federal government. As an independent sovereign entity, the Nagchaw Tribal Council oversees the Tribal Police Department, first-responders and emergency medical services, and court systems to protect their members and maintain law and order. In addition, education, workforce development, healthcare, social services, land and infrastructure systems management, building and other such programs fall under the authority of tribal governance.

The challenge that all such tribal entities face is keeping up with the needs of the population they serve. The Nagchaw Tribal Council had identified four areas that they were most concerned about and wanted to address for their members: 1) Unemployment, 2) Educational Opportunities, 3) Integrating into primary healthcare the support for substance abuse recovery, and most importantly, 4) the revitalization of their tribal language, customs, and traditions.

The twelve-person Tribal Council was split down the middle with the four identified concerns. Half of the council felt job development was most important, while the other half felt that education was the top priority, stating that jobs would follow if the population was properly educated. I took the position that both were equally important; some individuals were not destined to continue their formal education and would need jobs allowing them to earn an income. Others would benefit from skills training programs, such as Job Corps, and still others would be suited to go onto a community college or state university. This position eventually became the accepted view and was my first successful advisory stance while filling in on the council.

The inclusion of mental health services focused on substance recovery support was being tackled by Mike Milton who was making progress. The innovative programs at Thunder Road Recovery were allowing a variety of needs to be met and the council had been very impressed with what was happening. The Community Outreach Internship program was a glowing example of successful, innovative programming. Individuals were screened, interviewed, and then obtained their Drug and Alcohol Recovery Certificate at a nearby community college. Once their certificates were obtained and their internship hours fulfilled, participants graduated with a full-time or part-time job as a Thunder Road Outreach staff member. In fact, three of the council members had grandchildren who had graduated and were now employed as outreach workers with Thunder Road Recovery.

That left the last item, the loss of their traditional River People dialect, or Uto-Astecan language, and the Nagchaw customs and traditions, which for the entire council was a grave concern. There had been much discussion around how to rekindle interest in cultural restoration with a focus on working through the pain of historical trauma. This was a heated topic and the conversations that had been ongoing for months had begun to feel like a circular argument.

The Nagchaw Community Center housed the Tribal Council's meeting room and offices on the second floor, but the first floor was severely underutilized. It was thought that with the right kind of creative leadership that space offered the perfect location for just such a program. The council agreed that cultural restoration would need a strong center director who understood the need for an educational program with a creative arts component. This person would need to be tribe affiliated and have a background and degree in Native American studies.

Currently, there was no one on the reservation that met the three-fold criteria. There had been lively discussion around removing the educational requirement, but the council was split right down the middle on that. Half of the council felt adding the degree in Native American studies was asking too much, but the other half felt that it was necessary to set a precedent and keep the standard high for this position.

I couldn't help but think that this would be an excellent direction for Joslin. She had been talking with Mike Milton about the Native American Studies program at the U of A. In addition, she had recently spoken with an educational advisor, so Mike said. Having done so, I was hopeful that Joslin would pursue that program or the one at A.S.U. and that would certainly make her a prime candidate.

"So, Jos, sounds like you and Mike have been going over the pros and cons of applying to the U. of A.? You know Jos, Mike's hardly objective about the U. of A. since he attended their public health grad program. You might want to consider A.S.U. too, since they also have an indigenous studies program," I said.

"Oh okay, I see, then you're a completely objective A.S.U. alumni?" Joslin said, laughing at my not-so-subtle attempt at swaying her consideration toward my alma mater.

"You know Keith, I've been looking at the U of A's Native American Studies program for a while now. I haven't said anything since I know Dad would have a fit. I also applied for a scholarship, so he can't complain about any of his money being used for the program. I know you remember what a fit he threw when I enrolled at the Arizona School of Creative Arts!" Joslin said.

"Really, Sister, you're a surprise a minute these days, aren't you?"

"Maybe, but after our evening walks, and talks, along the Snake River about your experience with the medicine circles, sweats, and the men's drumming circle, I started thinking that studying our history would help me to feel more connected and more Nagchaw," Joslin said. "I know that I have the blood of our ancestors flowing through my veins, but I still get hung up on appearances. I just wish I looked more like you and Mom. Then I wouldn't feel like such a fraud as far as claiming to be Nagchaw," Joslin continued, blushing.

"Hey, listen, do you remember Stevie Bahe from high school?" I asked.

"Yes, I do. Why?"

"If I asked you to describe Stevie, without using a physical description, what would you say?"

"Oh, wow Keith, that's hardly a fair comparison. Yes, I know that Stevie was mixed and grew up on Nagchaw with his father's clan."

"Stop and don't avoid the question, Sister. Give me an answer, now, please."

"Okay, okay, without a doubt Stevie is a Nagchaw, a warrior, no wait...he's a Nagchaw warrior through and through. He's a lot like his father, Mom says. And he didn't have to live with this non-native parent constantly putting down the tribe and their traditions either," Joslin said. "But I get your point, although he looks more like his non-native mother there's no way Stevie's not Nagchaw. It's like he carries that energy, and it radiates off him." Joslin paused. "Okay, okay, I get it, it's totally in my head, in the way I think that has not allowed me to claim my ancestry. Which, by the way, is why I think being a part of a Native American Studies program will help me tackle that challenge," she said firmly. "With my B.A. from the Arizona School of the Arts, it's onward and upward to the U of A which seems like the logical next step, I do believe," she continued sounding excited.

When things are supposed to work out, they do. It's like Great Spirit has a plan and once we peons finally let go, the things that were meant to be come to fruition. I felt certain that Joslin's scholarship to the University of Arizona's Native American Studies program would happen. It wouldn't be a shock really, by the time she graduated from Coleman High her 3.7 GPA had skipped to a solid 4.0. And at the Arizona School for the Arts, she of course maintained that 4.0 GPA and made the Dean's Honor Roll each year.

Jos would bring her creativity to any program. Her senior project at the Arizona School for the Arts was a multicultural middle school program. This program allowed students to create stories illustrating aspects of their family genealogies. The students were then asked to identify the benefits of diversity within the communities from which they came. These kinds of opportunities seemed to be just the medicine my little sister needed to come out of her shell. I also couldn't help but think that being away from home, for obvious reasons, would help her bloom like the radiant sunflower I always knew she was.

Chapter 7

A Turbulent Wind

And yet when all has been said, we also know that oppor-
tunities for change are presented when we are ready.

Author: William Bridges, from *Transitions*

My time filling in on the Tribal Council had proved productive beyond my wildest dreams. In the beginning, out of respect for Mike Milton, who was the person the council originally wanted, my presence was tolerated. As time passed and I was helpful in establishing a handful of decisions, I was being given a serious second look.

I'd been kept abreast of the council's internal chatter by Lucy Keeton. Lucy told me that there was reason to believe that Nate Kylie might not be able to return to his council seat. The Tribal Council's Chief Executive had been unofficially meeting with each council member to ask for their assessment of my time as a council fill-in. Lucy said that the Tribal Council bylaws had an emergency provision for adding a new council member without going through the election process. Apparently, my time as a council fill-in met the criteria for being placed in that council seat, the caveat being there needed to be unanimous agreement of active council members, which was why Jericho Jefferson met individually to query opinions about my placement potential.

The chief executive, Jericho Jefferson, was well-known and much respected on Nagchaw and in Coleman too. He was a born leader and came to the reservation at a time of crisis when a strong leader was much needed. I had always respected Jericho, and for some odd reason felt like he and I were kindred spirits. Perhaps because there had been rumors that years ago, before Marta Yellowbird met and married Sam Gentry, Jericho Jefferson was widely considered to be the man my mother would have married. Still, he seemed to have no resentment toward me or my family, although like most folks on Nagchaw, he was not a fan of Sam Gentry.

I had received a call from Jericho asking to meet with me "about council business" and we scheduled a time that afternoon at the Tribal Council office. I went upstairs to the second floor and was warmly greeted by the Tribal Council's office manager and secretary.

"Good afternoon Allie, Rachel, is he in yet?" I asked.

"Good afternoon, Keith, yes he's here. Go on in, he's waiting for you." Allie said.

Suddenly I began to feel anxious as my stomach started to churn. Why, I wondered was this happening. Walking down the little hallway to his office, I suddenly heard a voice say, "A turbulent wind has blown but you are not seated by chance." I stopped and stood there for a couple of seconds before turning to look behind me, but no one was there. Trying to make sense of what I heard, I then realized that I couldn't just keep standing in the middle of the hallway, so I went to his office door and knocked.

"Come in Keith," Jericho said through the door. We warmly greeted each other, and I stuck out my hand to shake his, but Jericho gave me a quick hug instead and motioned for me to sit down. "I'm glad you decided to meet with me. I know I didn't say much about why I wanted to see you, but some things are better left unsaid until a face to face can happen," Jericho said.

"Yes, that usually works best if it's important to not discuss it over the phone." Not knowing what else to say, I simply gave his statement approval knowing that he'd explain more fully why we were meeting.

"So, I don't know if you're aware of this, but Nate Kylie's medical situation has taken a turn for the worse and he's had to resign from his council seat. Doc Watson called me personally to support Nate's decision, so it's necessary. The rest of the council has been made aware, and I wanted you to know too," Jericho said.

"Wow, okay, I see. I was wondering how Nate was doing. Originally, I had been told that this fill-in position was going to be a couple of months, but that point is long gone."

"It's hard to guess about a time length when the variable is a person's health. In the beginning Nate wasn't sure himself, and the estimate of 3 months was as good a guess as any." He paused. "Nate Kylie's resignation was never expected, and we'd hoped that he'd return to his seat, but now, that's not going to happen. So, we must decide what to do about Nate's council seat. Normally, filling a council seat requires an election by Tribal members, but this situation is not normal. The tribal bylaws have a special provision allowing for seating to take place without an election, if certain criteria are met," Jericho said. "One of the provisions is that there be unanimous approval by the rest of the council when an individual has served as a temporary fill-in. If his or her efforts have been deemed beneficial to the tribe, this individual can be approved and officially seated on the council."

"Okay, then, I'd guess my situation has met some of the criteria," I said.

"Oh, I'd say more than some of the criteria. I've spoken with each of the council members and unanimously it has been agreed upon that you, Keith Gentry, are the logical selection to fill Nate Kylie's council seat, if you'll have it."

I immediately thought about the words I heard before entering, *"A turbulent wind has blown but you are not seated by chance,"* and I clearly understood the message's meaning in this context.

"I must admit that I've wanted to be a part of the tribe's decision-making body for a while now, but I had never expected that it would happen this way. I'm honored to be asked to fill Nate's seat, and yes, I accept this offer," I said, elated. That weekend was filled with informal celebrations with family and friends. I, Keith Gentry, was now officially a council member on the Nagchaw Tribal governing body. I deeply felt that this was, in part, what my dreams had been foretelling and I was thrilled beyond belief.

Sam didn't say much about it at all. Under his breath, he congratulated me, but didn't make eye contact. I knew how he really felt about it, and I wasn't surprised in the least. As for my mother, Jos, Pawpaw, Grandma Moon, Mike, Telrica, and others, they were all excited for me. To celebrate, Jos made a dinner reservation at my favorite restaurant, Matta's, that Saturday evening. Sam said he would go, but at the last minute, apparently some odd construction emergency happened, so he wasn't able to attend the dinner celebration. I knew better, as did Marta and Jos. We went anyway as cancelling was not an option.

Besides, I was long overdue for my favorite Matta's dish, their chile rellenos. This was a delicious Poblano chili stuffed with a meat mixture, coated with egg, and covered with the most delicious green sauce on this side of the Snake River. Considering myself a chile relleno connoisseur, I found Matta's Restaurant to have the absolute best chile rellenos! Yes, my mother and sister teased me saying that I was a chili relleno addict, and no, I never contemplated recovery.

My time on the council flew by in the blink of an eye. Before I knew it, it had been a couple of years that I had been on the Tribal Council. I, without trying, became the talk of the reservation. A light started to shine on me that I was not completely comfortable with.

Rumors had started circulating that Jericho Jefferson, after multiple consecutive terms as Executive Chief, was considering retirement. Most of the council were in their late 40's or early 50's and had other interests or businesses they would return to if they left their current council seat. None, it seemed, were interested in the Executive Chief position. There was much talk about someone younger filling the position and trying to attract younger tribal members to run for council seats as they became available.

Pawpaw had been meeting with me for lunch every couple of weeks. We were meeting at Naturally Native, a little breakfast and lunch café. Besides being near the office, they were well known for serving the best Indian tacos this side of Tucson. "Grandson, how are you? How's everything going with your hot shot job these days?" Pawpaw asked as he took a bite of an Indian taco.

"Good Pawpaw, except I keep hearing rumors that Jericho Jefferson might be retiring in the next few months. Have you heard anything about that, Pawpaw?" I asked.

"No, I have not. Why do you ask?" Pawpaw said.

"Well, I keep hearing about him wanting to retire and then whispers about me being his logical replacement. You know, I really don't have enough experience to take on that position just yet."

"I take it you haven't spoken to Jericho about this."

"No, I haven't, and I know I probably should, but I've been hesitant for some reason," I admitted.

"Grandson, has your mother ever told you about her and Jericho back before she married Sam?" Pawpaw asked. "No, she's never really talked about it. I asked her once a long time ago after hearing about their history, but it didn't seem like she wanted to talk about it. I figured that maybe he broke her heart?"

"Maybe, but I don't think so. We were all hopeful that she was going to marry Jericho, but Sam entered the picture and unfortunately, the whole story changed," Pawpaw said. "I don't know what happened, but Marta and Jericho were such a good match. Your grandmother had arranged their meeting at the Tucson Powwow. They met and it seemed to be a good match. Everything seemed to be moving in that special direction, the direction of tying the knot, as they call it. He didn't have a lot in those days, but we could all see that he would become someone important. If only your mother hadn't fallen prey to the false charms of Sam Gentry," Pawpaw said sounding slightly angry.

"Yeah, having a father like Jericho would have been too good to be true. I mean, I never felt like Sam really cared that much about me. We've just never had much of a father-son connection. Jos has a better relationship with him than I do."

"Well, there might be a good reason why. You should ask your mother about Jericho again, sometime, try and get her to talk. You know, about how things were between her and Jericho back then," Pawpaw said.

I distinctly got the impression that Pawpaw had more to say, but for some reason he chose to stop there. I wondered what the issue might be involving the three of them. I got a sudden flood of intense emotions that flashed like pictures of a fast- moving slide show. I couldn't make any sense of them, except that they were with Jericho, my mother, and Sam. It was weird and it left me feeling like there was more to the very short story that I'd been told so long ago.

As we finished our lunch, Pawpaw invited me to come to a sweat ceremony that he would be attending.

"Grandson, the men on the Council of Elders are holding a sweat this weekend. Why don't you join us? As my grandson, you are welcome to come, if you can handle sweating with a bunch of old men," Pawpaw said, slightly laughing.

"Okay, I don't think Telrica, and I have anything going on this weekend, so yes, I'll be there," I answered, as we finished lunch.

I said good-bye to Pawpaw, we hugged, and went our separate ways. The walk back to the Tribal office was uncomfortable. It wasn't from the lunch we just ate, or the gust of hot wind that blew dust everywhere, but the conversation we had about Mom before she married Sam. It sparked an interest for me in knowing about what secrets Marta Yellowbird and Jericho Jefferson might have held onto for all these years.

Chapter 8

Spirit Dreaming

Many indigenous cultures have an intimate relationship with the dream world. They purposely work with their dreams as part of their everyday life to connect with the Great Mystery and the spirit realm. The dream world is available to anyone. Some people find meaning in their dreams and some dreams find the people who need meaning.

Author: Doug Good Feather, from *Think Indigenous*

On Sunday morning I dressed in loose fitting clothes and walked to the sweat lodge where Pawpaw met me. On the ground outside the lodge, I saw the fire pit where rocks were being heated as the firekeeper turned them. Before entering, Pawpaw smudged me by moving the smoke rising from the burning bowl with a large eagle feather from the top of my head down the length of my body and back up again.

Going inside, I placed my offering of tobacco into the woven basket next to the entrance. Looking around at those sitting in the circle, my presence was acknowledged with a nod. I took a seat on a cushion on the ground in the circle of elders. Closing my eyes, I settled my breathing and quieted my mind in preparation for things to come.

The firekeeper entered and placed heated rocks in the center pit. Pawpaw took a ladle from a wooden bucket filled with water and poured it over the heated rocks, creating steam which filled the lodge.

We sat in silence for the first few minutes and then Pawpaw spoke, blessing us and speaking the intentions of the sweat into existence.

"Now, we come together with open hearts and minds, so that the wisdom of the Ancients can make itself known. We ask that clarity and insight be present for all here. We ask that obstacles be cleared away, so that anything which we need to know, see, or hear will make itself known. Great Spirit, protect us from harm in all its forms and allow the intentions of those present to soar like the great eagle. *A'ho.*"

As the lodge filled with steam, I could feel toxins being released as my body was being purified. The elders chanted for a good while and then we sat in silence. My mind grew quiet, and I sat in silence for I don't know how long before anything happened. Then, as clear as day, I heard my name being called from a distance, from what seemed to be some faraway place. As I listened intently, I heard a voice say...

Keith, hear now the truth of your soul. Awaken from your deep sleep. Your spirit soars with the brown eagle since your birth. You are the anointed son of he who knows your heart. Know this truth.

As soon as this message ended, I jerked back into this time and was mesmerized by what I'd heard. I looked around and saw Pawpaw looking at me as he poured a ladle of water onto the rocks which again filled the lodge with steam. No longer able to see Pawpaw's face, I closed my eyes and sat in silence for I'm not sure how long. Then, Pawpaw closed our gathering with a prayer.

"Great Spirit, we thank you for allowing us to walk the red road with honor. Bless these men, your warriors, and give them the strength to follow any guidance from the visions, and messages received today. Bless their families and the Nagchaw reservation on which our Ancestors have always been one with Mother Earth. *A'ho.*"

As the sweat ended, I left the lodge with the others. When we entered the lodge, the morning sun was ascending and now it was nearing a high point in the sky. Outside, Grandma Moon was waiting with a large pitcher of herbal tea made from her home- grown herbs. Cups were passed to me and each elder before she left. As we sat outside quietly drinking the herbal tea, an elder shared what he experienced. I had always understood that receiving messages from the spirit world often takes the form of a vision... or perhaps an auditory message, as I had experienced.

I believe that dreams hold immense power as messengers from the spirit world by way of offering guidance, wisdom, and even warnings of things to come; however, my message had baffled me. I was hard pressed to make any sense of it, especially the reference to being the son of someone who knows my heart. What the heck did that mean? The message certainly wasn't referencing Sam. So, who was this message speaking about, I wondered.

I decided that I'd share what I heard with Pawpaw later,maybe at one of our Naturally Native lunch meetings. I hoped he would have some idea about what the meaning of that message was.

The following week was a busy one for the Tribal Council. Monday morning, Jericho called a short staff meeting which we were all expected to attend. I got to the conference room early and found Jericho sitting at the head of the table with a pile of papers spread out in front of him.

"Hey Jericho, looks like you started the meeting early," I said.

"Naw, I've got a backlog of paperwork to catch up on,which was why I wasn't at the sweat on Sunday." "Oh, you're a part of the elder council?" I asked.

"Yes, I've sat with the elders for a few years now. It's an honor to sweat with your grandfather. I always did like Pawpaw Yellowbird a lot," Jericho said.

"So, it sounds like you know some of my family well, which makes sense. After all, I hear you've got some Yellowbird history, yeah?" I asked.

"Oh, so your mother has mentioned me, has she?" Jericho chuckled.

"Not really. I asked her about you once, a long time ago, but it seemed like she didn't want to talk about it. You must have broken her heart badly back in the day."

"Oh yeah, sure, I broke her heart, that's a laugh," Jericho said and then looked like he regretted making that comment. "Sorry Keith, it's water under the bridge from many years ago. Your mom, Marta Yellowbird, is still very special to me." Jericho said.

At that moment, Lucy Keeton and the other council members filed into the conference room and our conversation stopped. I was left with the distinct feeling that had this opportunity not been cut short, I might have found out more about his water under the bridge history with my mother. I made a mental note to mention this conversation to Pawpaw the next time we met for lunch.

Later that day, I got a call from Pawpaw asking about lunch, so we met at Naturally Native café the next day, which was fast becoming our regular Indian Taco Tuesday.

"So, I was wondering how the sweat went for you, Grandson."

"Well, that's hard to say. I felt the presence of Great Spirit during the sweat, but I really didn't understand what the message I heard meant."

"Oh yeah? So Great Spirit spoke to you? Do you remember what the message was? What the exact words were?" Pawpaw asked.

"Pawpaw, I'll never forget these words. They're engraved into my mind, it seems. I can't stop thinking about what I heard. First, as clear as day, I heard my name spoken and then... *"Awaken from your deep sleep. Hear now the truth of your soul. Your spirit soars with the brown eagle since your birth. You are the anointed son of he who knows your heart. Know this truth."*

"Whoa Grandson, that's some powerful message."

"Yeah, I understand the brown eagle part. That's been a strange memory, dream, or vision that I've had since I was a baby.

It's hard to explain how that could be, but I carry that memory with me to this day. It's that other part that kind of freaks me out. What the heck does that last part mean? Whose anointed son am I? I mean, it sure doesn't sound like Sam Gentry, now does it?" I said, shaking my head.

Pawpaw sat silent, looking at me as if he wanted to say something, but he kept quiet. Sitting with Pawpaw I immediately thought about my interrupted conversation with Jericho before our staff meeting. I wanted to tell Pawpaw about what he'd said, but suddenly I felt unsure if I should say anything to him about that. It was all so confusing, and I wondered what the real story of Marta Yellowbird and Jericho Jefferson was. I felt that Pawpaw was carrying some burden, some heavy load that he wanted to share, but could not. I pleaded with him to talk to me, but he just sat and shook his head, and would only say "Speak with your mother."

Chapter 9

My Other Heritage

I salute the light within your eyes where the whole Universe dwells. For when you are at that center within you and I am at that place within me, we shall be one.

-- Crazy Horse

Several weeks had passed since Pawpaw urged me to speak with my mother again. Neither of us broached the subject when we met for lunch. I had pondered the possibilities of their history. From what I knew of Jericho, he had always been a well- respected member of the tribe and considered a "real catch" in his earlier days. Sometime later, he had been married to Sarah Whitewater, but only briefly as she had passed away from cancer. He had no children and I wondered why he never remarried. There were several women on the reservation that would have jumped at the chance of marrying such an outstanding member of the tribe. Knowing all of this, I had a burning desire to find out what the story behind his and Mom's history was before he left office. Jericho was just so different from Sam I was genuinely perplexed as to why my mother would have married Sam and not Jericho.

I found Jericho Jefferson to be an excellent supervisor. He was direct in his communication, clear on his expectations, and honest with his feedback. Having had other kinds of supervisors, I was clearly able to recognize how lucky I was in this situation.

We had a better than average relationship, compared to other council members, and I recognized that. I knew he saw me as a potential successor to the Tribal Council Chief Executive position upon his retirement. I'd gotten comfortable with that. After I had been officially seated as Nate Kylies' replacement, Jericho unofficially took me under his wing. He began showing me the ropes, as the saying goes. He stated that he'd finish his current term, which was up in 8 months. Although he'd stated that he'd be available by way of the advisory board, I preferred having direct contact with him.

"Keith, are you free for lunch today?" Jericho asked. "Sure, I was just thinking about that," I said.

"Yeah, I thought so, I can hear your stomach growling," Jericho said as we laughed. "Let's go now, since the lunch crowd should be over at the café."

Our walk to Naturally Native was only three blocks. The fall weather was mild, and it was a great day for walking. Our conversation on the way to the café was light, about Jericho's favorite NFL team and player, the Pittsburg Steelers and running back Franko Harris. He was right about the timing for lunch, the café was empty. We sat and ordered our food. We continued our conversation about the Steeler's and Franko for a few minutes more before Jericho changed the subject.

"So, Keith, how's your mother these days? Is she still growing her medicinal herbs?" Jericho asked.

"Yes, she is, she still likes to use her natural remedies whenever given the chance. She's always been an herbalist at heart," I said. "You know, Jericho, I don't want to pry, but I've been curious about what your relationship with Mom was like before she married Sam."

"Hmm, I thought that Marta would have told you about that. Oh wait, that's right, you said she avoided talking about it." He paused. "I guess it's still too uncomfortable of a subject for her, which is interesting. Back then, I was the one who had the hard time accepting her decision."

"Oh, so she, broke your heart? I thought it was the other way around, from the way she avoided talking about it. There's never been much that she wouldn't talk to me about, except that," I said.

"Yeah, well, your mother and I had an intense love affair. I thought we were happy during the time we were together. Just when I thought we'd be getting married, she broke it off, and shortly thereafter married Sam. It took me a long time to get over her. In some ways, I never have," Jericho said, looking forlorn. "I'm so sorry that happened, Jericho. I didn't mean to pry, but I've wondered for years about why you two didn't marry."

"That's the greatest unanswered question of my life. No, not in a million years will I ever understand why she chose Sam over me."

At that point our conversation went back to football, and I had to push myself not to keep asking questions about their history.

The next day was Indian Taco Tuesday, and I met Pawpaw for lunch. I wondered if I should tell him about my conversation with Jericho. I went back and forth and then decided to tell Pawpaw and see what his take was on what he said.

"Nothing you've shared about what Jericho said is new to me Grandson. The entire tribe was just as shocked as he was with what happened. And that's a fact. Your grandmother and I both tried to sway your mother back into her right mind, but she wouldn't have it. You know how stubborn your mother can be when she's made her mind up. She's just like your grandmother when it comes to that," Pawpaw said, laughing. "There was something else going on in their situation back then. We couldn't get your mother to speak about whatever it was. It drove your grandmother and I crazy. Whatever it was, your mother has held onto it, to this day. I guess it's the secret that she'll take with her into the spirit world," Pawpaw said.

"Do you think Jericho was treating her badly? Abusing her, or something like that?" I asked.

"Oh no. No, I'm sure that wasn't it. Jericho is an honorable man and he'd never do anything like that. He truly worshipped the ground your mother walked on, which is why it was so shocking that she broke up with him. It took a long time for him to get over your mother," Pawpaw said.

"Yeah, that's what he said too. I felt so bad for him when he was telling me about it. It was like I could feel his pain."

I wondered what the issue was that Pawpaw was referring to. It must have been something important if both of her parents were concerned and trying to persuade her to talk about it.

That weekend, I met up with Sis, as we took our walk along the Snake River. I told her about my conversation with Jericho and then Pawpaw. Joslin was genuinely surprised; she never really knew that there'd been anyone other than Sam our mother had been with.

"Gosh, I find it strange to think about Mom with anyone else. I mean, she just doesn't seem like someone who would have dated much to me, but Grandma has made comments over the years about her. These comments always seemed like she was talking about someone else. You know, someone more spirited, and full of life. Of course, after so many years people do change. Especially after living with someone like our father," Joslin said, looking bleak.

Yes, being married to Sam Gentry has taken a toll on our mother. I would have given anything to have been able to convince her to leave him and move back onto the Rez where her family would receive her with open arms. Even so, I believe her fear of what he might do has been enough to keep her in Coleman. Still, I know that the day will come when our mother, Marta Gentry will stand up and become Marta Yellowbird once again. Mark my word, when that happens, she'll not think twice about leaving and there will be no opposing her decision once she's made up her mind. I only hope that I will be there to escort her back to Nagchaw.

The following week Mike Milton asked me to pick up another support group at Thunder Road. He'd started a group with elderly men on the reservation who were struggling with sobriety and needed extra support to stick with the recovery process. With the younger men in my group, that process involved supporting their recovery by developing coping skills and learning to manage cravings. My goal was to enhance their motivation to get clean and stay sober.

With this group of elderly men, I needed to work a little differently. I was going to encourage them to support and help each other through the recovery process as a strategy to reduce symptoms of depression and isolation as well as increase their overall satisfaction with life. These men had all spoken with Mike and agreed to give the recovery group a try. Mike had asked each man to commit to coming weekly for two months. A couple of them objected to such a long trial period, but in the end all had given their word to do that.

The Council of Elders was a revered group on Nagchaw. These elders were honored and respected by the tribe and were considered important keepers of traditions as well as the oral history of the Nagchaw. Pawpaw was on this council and a much respected elder on Nagchaw, as was Grandma Moon.

This group of elder men were not a part of this council. Most, if not all, had a history of run-ins with the law in Coleman and a few had spent time in county jail and two in the state facility. The fact that they felt that they had dishonored their families, and the tribe was a huge impediment to their ability to stay sober. Self-forgiveness would be a focus to reestablish their sense of belonging and being an elder worthy of the respect of the tribe.

Personally, I found facilitating these groups helpful for my own sense of wellbeing. Having had a father who didn't respect my existence gave me a foot in the door as far as how many of these men felt. I understood the need to be valued and respected for simply being who I was. I understood what these men were struggling with and what their needs were.

It was about two months into the weekly support meetings with the elders when Ben Williams began talking about his personal history and how he had trouble sleeping for what seemed like years. After the group had finished, all the participants had left except Ben. He was helping me put up the folding chairs, and as we were finishing, he asked me a question that floored me.

"Hey, Keith, how'd you get so good at all this group stuff anyway?' he asked.

"Well, I did an internship at a recovery program in Phoenix when I was going to school. I was in a business program, but I also took classes on human development and psychology too," I said.

"So, you don't think you got any of your skills from your dad? He was always so good with understanding us hardheaded Indians, you know?" he said.

"Oh, wow, I never considered that Sam liked much less understood me or any of the hardheaded ones on Nagchaw."

"Naw, I ain't talking about that ignorant fool. I'm talking about your real father, the one who you look like, the one who you remind me so much of," he said. "What?" Shocked, I stood there frozen looking at Ben wondering why he said that.

"Oh, man, sorry. I just always assumed that you were his son. I think a lot of people here on the Rez have that thought too. It was such a big shock when your Mom broke it off with him and then turned around and married Sam. But now days nobody speaks about that, especially after so long."

Still in a state of shock, I hardly knew what to say. Since I'd moved onto the Rez, there had been times that folks my mom's age or older had commented about how I reminded them of a young Jericho Jefferson, but I didn't think twice about it then. Then, I hadn't really considered that it could even be a possibility, but now, I wondered. Could it be true? Might Jericho really be my biological father? Is that what's behind Sam's coldhearted feelings towards me? Is that why my own mother won't speak with me at all about her history with Jericho? I staggered to the last chair not yet folded up and sat down. Then Ben came over to me and pulled a folding chair off the rack and sat down in front of me.

"Man, Keith, I'm sorry for saying that. I have no proof, other than what my eyes tell me. And you know how unreliable our vision is about this kind of thing," Ben said laughing. "It's been a question many folks on the Rez have pondered over the years. When your mom married Sam and moved off the Rez, some of the women were saying that she was already pregnant. Maybe she didn't know it for sure back then. Still, it's all talk, just busybody talk. You know how gossip is with some folks, yeah?" Ben asked.

Not wanting to continue this conversation, I told Ben not to worry, that I was sure that wasn't the case. Yes, I drew the short stick and got Sam Gentry as my father. Ben laughed and acknowledged that having Sam as a father would be because I drew the shortest stick of the lot. We put up the last two chairs and walked out to the front and into the parking lot. We shook hands and said our goodbyes as I turned and walked back to the Tribal Council office. There was much work to be done and I was going to put this thought on the back burner for now. Further down the road when it seemed appropriate to question my mother and Jericho more fully about that as a possibility, I would.

Chapter 10
The Truth of History

According to department records, one in three Native American women are raped during their lifetimes—two-and-a-half times the likelihood for an average American woman—and in 86 percent of these cases, the assailant is non-Indian.

"On Indian Land, Criminals Can Get Away with Almost Anything" by Sierra Crane-Murdoch, *The Atlantic*

The next few months were intense. All the usual business of governing the tribe was being attended to along with several service- related contracts that were coming due; however, the icing on the cake was what happened one Saturday night. This Saturday night, Coleman's Mayor Winston's son Louis, after drinking heavily, left The 5th Amendment, a little dive bar on the outskirts of town. He picked up a hitch hiker who happened to be an underaged Nagchaw female half his age. Instead of taking this underaged female home, he took her down the old back road along the Snake River. This location had a reputation for being the spot to party and the spot for those wanting privacy for illicit excursions. This area was technically on the reservation, but most folks weren't aware of that since the signs that had been posted stating "Nagchaw Reservation" were routinely pulled down so that those who were frequent trespassers could claim "We didn't see any signs posted officer!"

While patrolling the area, the Tribal Police came across Louis Winston and the Nagchaw girl half-dressed on a makeshift mattress in the bed of his pickup. These kinds of situations were known for putting the Tribal Police in a very ill-tempered mood. In fact, once they realized that they had the mayor's son, they threw the book at him. He was handcuffed, taken to Nagchaw PD, and thrown into a holding cell. His one phone call was, of course, made to his father, Mayor Winston. The mayor drove out to the Rez at one o'clock in the morning and spent 30 minutes in Captain Batton's office. The yelling and screaming by both men was loud enough to be heard on the main office floor.

Because the young girl refused to press charges, the mayor's son got off with a warning, which should have made Mayor Winston happy, but instead he looked to get even with things to come.

The following month, in retaliation, the City of Coleman revoked a Nagchaw contract given the nasty political fallout involving Louis that night. The revoked contract created supply chain issues, and nobody was happy about the disruption of necessary equipment and supplies coming into the Native American Health Center.

For the next few weeks there was much talk around the Rez about Mayor Winston's son getting away with something that he should have been punished for. As tribal members were filing into the office to express their outrage and file formal complaints about the conclusion of that incident, Jericho assigned me to meet individually with the complainants.

"So, Keith, our people aren't happy about the situation with the mayor's son. This isn't the first time something like this has happened either. Our people know that tribal authorities cannot arrest and prosecute non-Natives who commit crimes on the reservation. All we can do is issue a traffic ticket, which was done for Louis parking his truck too near the river. Still, knowing that's the case, it's not right that all Mr. Winston got was a slap on the hand and told to be a good boy," Jericho said.

"It's another travesty of justice that needs to be addressed. And the reason that *I am not proud of that half of my heritage*," I said, watching Jerico's expression.

"Good Keith, because I want you to meet with anyone who comes in to file a formal complaint. There's no outright solution, but you can listen and be supportive. Encourage the complainants to talk with their young people about this. Make them aware of the reality of the situation. Then document the complaint on the NTC form at the front desk," Jericho said.

"I guess this is a perfect example of why the council's been looking to hire a director for the community center. This is easily an area where youth workshops about knowing their rights would be in line with a cultural restoration focus," I said.

"Yes, there's been some on-Rez interest, but we haven't found anyone with the tri-combo background. We have plenty of folks here who are registered members of the tribe, but none of them the have a degree in Native American Studies, or a creative arts background. I believe the combo is important and my gut tells me there's someone out there who just hasn't found us yet," Jericho said.

It was this conversation that got me thinking again about my sister, Joslin, for this position. She had two of the three and was leaning toward registering for the U of A's Native American Studies program. She could do her internship on the Rez and begin setting up a program. It all made sense to me, but would it make sense to Joslin?

I won't lie, completing Jericho's assignment of meeting with tribal members and taking their formal complaints about the Louis Winston incident was rough. By the end of week three, I was ready to burn Coleman to the ground. Yet, I could not say that or act unprofessional in any way while listening and documenting their complaints.

At the end of the week, I stopped by The Scarab, a local watering hole for a cold beer before heading home. I entered and walked the length of the bar looking for an open bar stool. Luckily, I found a spot near the end of the ole red cedar bar. The bartender, Tim McGee, was a gangly redhead with freckles who also waited tables at Matta's. Tim greeted me as I sat down and asked, "A Corona?" As soon as I took that first sip, I heard a semi-familiar voice that immediately caused an uneasy feeling in the pit of my stomach.

"Hey, it's high school Indian dude! Look at you, all gussied up coming in after your cushy job on the Rez! Damn, you lazy Indians have it easy, don't you?" Why is it that some people are never satisfied until they feel superior to you. That certainly seemed the case with my old high school nemesis, Jack Mitchell, the former Coleman High football star. Now Jack worked for Sam as a construction laborer and could frequently be found drinking at the 5th Amendment, where patrons had questionable reputations, to say the least.

I did my best to ignore Jack since it was obvious that he was drunk, but when he walked up to my barstool, I had to address him.

"Look Jack, you're drunk, so go back to your seat. We're not going to get into it this evening, so go now, and leave me alone."

Jack walked back to his seat not far from where I was and then said...

"Aww, now, did that hot little Indian bitch you've been seeing kick you to the curb? I'll just bet you had trouble satisfying her," Jack said laughing hysterically.

With that comment, I immediately reacted by getting up and walking directly over to Jack, who got up just as I approached. Before he could say anything, I punched him in the face, knocking him out cold. To my surprise, my punch was met with loud cheers and clapping by the patrons, and shortly thereafter the bar owner approached me.

"Look, Keith, I'm so sorry, don't worry about the beer, it's on the house. You know this ornery SOB will want to settle the score, so you had best go before he comes round. Again, I'm so sorry about this."

As I left The Scarab, a couple leaving the bar said that I should watch my back as Jack was known for getting revenge for such incidents. I replied that I would and thanked them. Honestly, the thought of spending any more time thinking about Jack was an irritant that I planned to avoid at all costs.

Chapter 11

A Final Curtain Call

Bravery involves a willingness to let our defenses and hiding places be exposed, so that we can open more fully to life. To be a warrior in a relationship means being willing to face our pain and fear, instead of always trying to avoid them.

Author: John Welwood, Ph.D.
from *Love and Awakening*

Writing a scene and putting it on paper is one thing but bringing that scene to life through an actor's interpretation is something else completely. Telrica believed that getting the right interpretation was extremely important. She always gave whatever production she was involved in her full and undivided attention from the beginning to the very end. It was the last night of the play *The Rising Tide* at the Theater of Performing Arts in Tucson. Jos and I sat in the third row from the front. We were equally dazzled from her first appearance on stage to the final curtain call, which was spectacular. At the curtain call, Telrica was presented with a dozen red roses as she bowed repeatedly waving to the cheering crowd which went on for a full five minutes. Afterwards, Jos and I waited in the lobby for our performing princess. While waiting we discussed her talent, which quite frankly didn't surprise either of us. To know Telrica was to understand how delighted she was to embrace a role and then bask in the spotlight when she was successful. In the theater as in life, she swept her audience and her admirers off their feet and held them in her clutches until she decided to let go. Telrica was truly in her element on stage, and I had no doubt that it would be any different for her on a Hollywood big screen.

After dropping Jos off at the house, when we'd gotten back to her place, Telrica and I got into a heated conversation about her going to Hollywood. She was so excited and talking a mile a minute as if she'd already been discovered, found an agent, and landed a blockbuster movie deal. I wasn't feeling this conversation one bit. I didn't respond well, which got me into hot water, again. This area of our relationship had become more than contentious—it was downright volatile.

"Keith, I get that you aren't interested in Hollywood, but I am. I'm sorry but I don't find the Nagchaw Rez captivating enough to keep me here. I'd die if I had to stay in Coleman or on the Rez. There's nothing, just nothing here for me Keith. Why don't you understand that, damn it..." Telrica said with tears streaming down her face.

"Look, I get that, really I do. After seeing you onstage tonight, I'm fully convinced that

Hollywood is where you're headed. The thing is, I don't like to think about you leaving. I know it needs to happen, but still, it pisses me off to no end."

"Keith, that's so selfish! I don't believe that you can be angry about my leaving if you truly understand what acting means to me. How can you be so understanding and concerned 'bout the folks living on the Rez, and yet get pissed off about me leaving to fulfil a dream? Why? Tell me why Keith Gentry!" Telrica said, now yelling at me.

There was an uncomfortable silence that followed. Telrica went around her apartment slamming doors, cupboards, the refrigerator, and finally threw herself down on her bed with her face in her pillow. I knew better than to say anything without having thought it through. How could I explain exactly what I was feeling in a way that calmed her down and made her able to see my side?

I walked into her bedroom and sat down on the edge of her bed. Neither of us moved for a good five minutes, then she rolled over and sat up next to me.

"Sweetheart, if you gave up your dream and stayed here, I too believe you would die or go crazy. I know that the Rez, Coleman, none of it is enough for you. I really do know that, but there's something else I know. I know that you are someone very special to me. You fill a place in my heart that no one...yes, no one...has ever filled. You bring joy and pleasure to my life in a way that I've never had anyone do before, don't you understand that. You make me want to make things here, in Coleman, and on Nagchaw better. Not just for all the others, but for you. I can't explain why I need to stay here and do what I'm doing, just know that it's my calling, like acting is your calling," I said. After I finished, she turned slowly, hugged me, and then started to cry. She didn't need to say anything, because I could feel that she understood where I was coming from.

We talked for a while longer and we both promised to change the course of our conversations as far as talking about the future. The night turned to early morning as we got undressed and got into bed. Holding her in my arms, we both had a good laugh about being so tired as we drifted off to sleep.

A couple days later, I met Jos near the Snake River for our periodic check-in. As we walked along the path next to the river where we played as kids, I told her about the argument with Telrica and how it ended.

"You know she's important to me, but she's on her way to a whole other kind of life. She could never be happy in the long run staying in Coleman or on Nagchaw. She knows that I love her, but it's not enough to keep her here.

It's so sad, but I don't see us making it long term, Jos."

"Wow, I guess it makes sense though. Like we talked about that night while waiting for her in the lobby. She's been bitten by the acting bug, and nothing will satisfy her until she's on the big screen and the cover of People Magazine," Jos said.

"Yeah, that's about the sum of it, Jos. It just kills me to think about her leaving," I said.

No longer feeling like talking we continued walking along the pebble-laden path until we reached a certain point and then turned around and went back. It was getting hot, and it was a muggy morning as the monsoons were on their way. Jos tried her best to comfort me, she encouraged me to stick with the relationship until it ran its course, and "Who knows..." she said "...sometimes things don't turn out as we expect them to." I guess that remained to be seen. No matter what happens, Telrica Tusoni was and will always be the love of my life.

Chapter 12

The Way of Like Minds

Collective impact describes the process of finding your truth and being a part of a like-minded community. We elevate awareness and become a living example of truth in action.

Author: Doug Good Feather from *Think Indigenous*

Jericho Jefferson and I had begun having more and more discussions about activism and shining a light on crimes being perpetrated against the Nagchaw Nation. A byproduct of the Louis Winston incident with a minor for many on the Rez was a last straw. The Council of Elders had asked for a meeting with the Tribal Council and wanted something done. The concerns of those who filed formal complaints needed to be acknowledged as legitimate, and that would hopefully send a message that the situation was not hopeless.

Since Pawpaw was the informal leader of the Council of Elders, Jericho had asked that I sit next to him during that meeting instead of in Nate Kylie's old seat. He told me that being placed next to him was a visual cue that he knew the elder council would recognize and find value. There had been ample scuttlebutt around

Nagchaw about finding a replacement for Jericho before he retired. Although we had not yet had that conversation, I knew that it was coming.

"Thank you for this visit, Grandfather Yellowbird and esteemed elders. Your presence in the house of the Nagchaw is an honor and we are pleased that you are here. Please tell us how we can be of service," Jericho said.

"Thank you, Jericho and seated council members. We came here today to express our concerns about the upheaval caused by the incident with Mayor Winston's son. Although this kind of thing has happened before, this incident has stuck in the craw of many who want something done," Pawpaw said.

"Yes, I had assigned this important task of listening to and taking the complaints of our members to Keith. He has shared much about that experience with the council during our weekly meetings. Keith, will you please share with the elders council what you learned from that assignment?" Jericho asked.

Although caught off guard, I had considered that I might be asked about the interviews and what information I gathered from the complainants. Fortunately, I was primarily addressing Pawpaw, who was front and center, which was beneficial for having to speak on the fly at such an important meeting.

"In a nutshell, I can tell you this: Most of the complainants were already aware of the Supreme Court's selective justice ruling of a couple of years earlier. Having disallowed tribes to arrest and prosecute non-Natives who commit crimes on the reservation is the epitome of injustice. Still, what several of the complainants thought would be helpful would be to finally get someone into the center director spot downstairs. They've been hearing the term "cultural restoration" and feel that this would be the ideal setting to incorporate programs and workshops for our young people with a focus on knowing their rights. The well-being of our tribe is dependent upon instilling a sense of self-empowerment that leads to liberation from a historically unjust way of living under the white man's rule," I said.

A round of lively discourse ensued as everyone had an opportunity to express what they thought and how they felt. The meeting ended almost 90 minutes later. I could tell that Pawpaw and Jericho were more than pleased with what had transpired during our time together.

Our meeting with the Elder's Council took us well past our usual lunchtime. A few of the council members decided to take a break after the meeting and walk to Naturally Native for lunch. As we left the building and turned the corner, a late model black Chevy truck with a red hood and red pinstriping, along with tinted windows, sped around the corner coming right at us. Luckily the truck made so much noise we all saw it and quickly got out of the way. That near miss made me queasy, and I had an unsettled feeling about what had just happened. We were a group crossing a street that wasn't heavily trafficked, so that show of aggression felt personal to me. I hated to give the incident at The Scarab with Jack Mitchell any more thought, but I recalled the verbal warning I received from the couple leaving the bar at the same time. Was that Jack behind the wheel? Did he have the audacity to come onto the reservation to try and settle the score?

I wondered and some part of me knew that if that was Jack, I'd be seeing him again in the not-too-distant future.

We got to Naturally Native and sat in a large booth and placed our orders with Emmy Jane, the sweetest waitress on staff at this establishment.

"*Yá át tééh* council folks, whatcha havin' for lunch today?" Emmy Jane asked.

Emmy took our orders and then made a statement that almost made me lose my appetite.

"I hear y'all almost had a 10-57 on your way here? I don't know what that idiot was doing all morning, driving about like he was lost or looking for someone. You know how Jack Mitchell's like a dirty dog searching for his long-lost bone!" Emmy said as we laughed at her on-point description.

There it was. My confirmation that Jack would stay true to his nature. He'd look to get even for having been knocked out at The Scarab. I wondered if I should seek out Jack and try to settle it once and for all? After all, he'd been itching to do the same to me since high school. With someone like Jack there was no letting go of the need to settle a score, especially when he believed he didn't do anything to deserve such treatment. Plus, Jack was known to have a gun rack across his back truck window. That combo of a drinker with a loaded shotgun was not a winning combination. The only way I could legitimately handle this was to avoid him. I figured I'd need to take heed by looking over my shoulder, but you know, that really wasn't my style. I'd never had to live that way and I wasn't going to start doing that now.

As we wrapped up our lively lunch conversation, everyone reflected on a specific part of our session with the Elder's Council. There seemed to be a consensus that we needed to, once again, push forward with finding a person who could take the director's position downstairs in our building. When the structure was originally built, the intention was that the first floor would become an active cultural resource and preservation center as well as an educational meeting site. These resources would showcase the remnants of sites associated with our historical ancestors; this would include those aspects of the natural landscape that have a traditional cultural significance to the Nagchaw tribe.

The curriculum of the Nagchaw Cultural Center would be with an eye to the future for our young people: Reinstilling the traditional River People dialect, or Uto-Astecan language, and sacred traditions could be introduced by way of unique and creative integration with the arts. This would be the primary focus, integrating the ways of our ancestors, the Ancient Ones, by connecting art and our history, which has always been the path of the Nagchaw.

Walking back to the office, I couldn't stop envisioning Jos in that position. I knew with her astute mind she'd clearly understand the intention behind what the cultural arts center was to be. She'd been bitten by the Nagchaw bug too now and was clearly showing interest in learning about her cultural heritage. I made a mental note to myself to begin talking to her about all this on our check-in walks along Snake River. I know she'd be a fantastic center director, if given the chance.

Chapter 13

An Unexpected Pig in a Poke

Physical reality is not a dead and empty stage on which Life evolves. Every physical form, as well as every non-physical form, is Light that has been shaped by consciousness. No form exists apart from consciousness. Reality is a multilayered creation. No two people have the same reality.

Author: Gary Zukav from *Seat of the Soul*

He was a vision to behold, as he glided in through the door as smoothly as silk, or maybe a cool wind gust on an October evening during the monsoons. Charlie "Riptide" Cosay was tall, dark, handsome, and dressed to the nines. He wore a preppy button-down powder blue Oxford shirt, creased straight- leg denim jeans, with an Italian leather belt and loafers. He finished off his visual with an Omega wristwatch and generously applied English Leather aftershave. His long, thick black hair was neatly pulled back into a ponytail which hung to the middle of his back. He looked to be an Apache with his high cheekbones, well-formed nose, and strong jaw. His brown eyes were fiery hot with energy as he approached the Tribal Council's front desk receptionist. Rachel was awestruck and staring with her mouth hanging slightly open. As he said "hello," he bent down and looked right into her eyes as he shook her hand.

"Hello, how are you Miss...Miss...." Charlie paused. "Rachel, aww, Miss Rachel—how can I help you?" she said.

"Who's in charge around here? I'd like to speak with the big chief please. It's very important, it's about the financial future of this tribe, of the...the..." Charlie stammered. "The Nagchaw reservation?" Rachel asked.

"Yes indeed, the Nagchaw reservation. So, who'd you say was in charge? And when can I get in to speak with him?" Charlie asked.

"Wait here, I'll check to see if Jericho Jefferson, our Tribal Council Chief Executive is available. Who may I say is asking to see him?" Rachel asked.

"Tell him Mr. Charles Cosay requests a meeting about the financial future of the Nagchaw tribe. Please tell him that I'll require no more than 15 or 20 minutes of his valuable time," Charlie said.

Rachel tripped as she rounded the corner from her desk. She was visibly shaken and embarrassed by her clumsy-footed stumble as she got up to walk back to Jericho's office; a minute later she returned. "He said he can see you now, but he's only got 15 minutes before his next meeting," Rachel said.

"Okay, I'll take it," Charlie said.

"Right this way, sir."

"Oh Rachel, no need for such formalities. You, pretty lady, can call me Riptide. That's my nickname and only special people get to call me that." Charlie winked at her, as Rachel blushed.

As Charlie approached Jericho's office and knocked, he overheard me saying, "I know all about this Riptide guy. He's slick and he's got some kind of scam. He's already tried to pull it on our Northern brothers. Don't take this meeting with him Jericho, he's a fraud."

"Come in Mr. Cosay. How can I help you?" Jericho asked.

"Well, to start with you can hear me out before you listen to anyone who thinks they know what I'm about. If you would be so kind as to excuse this misinformed young man so we can talk freely." Charlie said, looking at me.

Walking past Charlie, I paused. I looked Charlie up and down and then directly into his eyes and said, "I know all about you Riptide," and walked out of Jericho's office closing the door behind him.

"Have a seat Mr. Cosay, please, and don't mind that young man, he's not familiar with our ways," Jericho said. smiling and looking at the wall clock.

"Okay, thank you. So, Mr. Jefferson, I only have one question for you. Are you, as the big boss around here, satisfied with the resources available to your tribal members? By resources I mean employment training programs, and how about educational opportunities? Your tribal members need good training programs so that they can go out and compete for decent paying jobs, right?" Charlie asked.

"Yes, increased employment training programs and educational opportunities are currently goals that our council is working on for our tribal members," Jericho said nodding and smiling.

"Well, Mr. Jefferson, I've got a fantastic investment opportunity that I'd like to share with you. This investment opportunity will easily bring a 50% return within 90 days! Imagine this, please, you'll make $2500 with your first $5000 investment within 90 days and the complete investment plus an additional 50% return in 180 days or 6 months. Imagine what you'll be able to do for the tribe with this kind of investment return. Imagine the things that you can make happen with the capital earned during these hard times. It's a real opportunity and a real chance to become the most successful Tribal Council Chief since who knows when!" Charlie said, laughing heartily while reaching over to shake Jericho's hand, except that right then Jericho pushed his chair back from his desk and stood up.

"Thank you Mr. Cosay, but I have another meeting to attend now. Before you go, I'd like to ask a favor of you, if you don't mind..." Jericho said, smiling at Charlie. "Sure, since we're going to be doing business together in the future, just ask." Charlie said.

"After you leave here and are driving off the reservation, please remember, DON'T EVER SHOW YOUR FACE HERE AGAIN UNLESS YOU WANT A 4-STAR ACCOMMODATION EXPERIENCE AT THE NAGCHAW TRIBAL POLICE STATION."

Surprised, Charlie got up from his seat and started to say something but then stopped. He looked at Jericho and realized that he had better leave without making a fuss or that 4-star accommodation might be where he'd be spending the night.

"Well then, Mr. Jefferson, not everyone is cut out for such a lucrative opportunity, so I will leave you now. Have a good day, and when you change your mind, please give me a call anytime." Charlie said, laying his business card upside down on his desk and then walking out of his office.

As Charlie walked down the hall and into the front lobby, he glanced sideways at Rachel and nodded as he walked out the door. Shortly thereafter Jericho walked out to the front lobby and spoke to Rachel.

"Rachel, the next time Charlie Cosay shows his face in this office, immediately notify me and then call Captain Batton. He'll send one of his officers over to escort Mr. Cosay off the reservation or maybe for an overnight stay in the holding cell." Jericho said.

As Jericho walked down the hall back into his office, he glanced at the business card Charlie left on his desk, and he picked it up. Turning the card over, he laughed out loud as he read the print which said:

> *Thank you for allowing me to speak with you today. Although I have a lucrative investment opportunity, I will not be lining your pockets with greenbacks! May you toss and turn in bed tonight as you realize your grave error in judgement! Sincerely, Charlie "Riptide" Cosay.*

A few minutes later, I and the other council members started taking our seats in the conference room next to Jericho's office. Before entering the conference room, Jericho stuck his head in and nodded for me to step out into the hallway for a minute.

"Boy Keith, you had his number alright! Riptide was ready to take as much as he could get out of the tribal coffers and leave this tribe broke and humiliated. It's not going to happen on my watch, or in the future...on your watch either, Keith," Jericho said.

The last part of Jericho's statement didn't go unnoticed. As we returned to the conference room to start the meeting, I felt slightly stunned. I had expected Jericho to eventually speak with me about my future on the council, but not by mentioning it so casually, as if it was a fully understood given.

Calling the meeting to order, Jericho addressed what had just happened with Charles "Riptide" Cosay with the council members.

"Good morning. Off the agenda, I'd like to briefly start by sharing what just took place here in my office. I just had an encounter with the worst kind of flimflammer. I say the worst because he was one of us. Not a Nagchaw, but probably a Chiricahua from the San Carlos Apache Nation. Charles "Riptide" Cosay came in full of promises about a lucrative investment opportunity which would make me the most 'successful' Tribal Chief Executive the Nagchaw Nation has ever seen, so he said. I listened and then promised him that if he ever showed his face on this reservation again, Captain Batton will have one of his officers escort him to the station and a holding cell for an overnight stay. We must always stay vigilant when speaking with those who promise lucrative investment returns for the future. I'm not sure if any of our brothers up north bought into his scam, but if so, we'll likely hear about it soon. Our duty to this office is to be mindful that these kinds of things happen all the time. Should you encounter any of our members who were scammed by Charlie or any other barracuda, our duty is to advise them how and where to report these frauds, scams, and bad business practices that impact their lives, families, and our tribe. Therefore, I will be reaching out to our state American Indian advocacy group and to Tribal legal aid inviting them here to speak with us. We need to become more familiar with what the resources are by way of the organizations that advocate for the rights and protection of our tribe. I'll let you know via email when I can get that scheduled. Now, onto the items on the agenda that you received coming into our meeting this morning."

Chapter 14
The Sound of Wind and Rain

Each interaction with every individual is part of a contin-ual learning dynamic. When you interact with another, illusion is part of this dynamic. This illusion allows each soul to perceive what it needs to understand in order to heal. It creates, like a living picture show, the situations that are necessary to bring into wholeness the aspects of each soul that requires healing.

Author: Gary Zukav from *Seat of the Soul*

I sat listening to the monsoon wind and rain outside while I waited for Sam to return home after work. Mom had left for Basha's to pick up some last-minute items for tonight's din-ner and then Joslin from the Coleman library. Her car wouldn't start, and she was certain that all it needed was a jump, but she didn't have a charging cable.

Sam had called me at work and asked to speak with me. He said he wanted to talk about the business and its future. I told him that I'd come over after work and stay for dinner, which made my mother more than happy. Both she and Joslin were always complaining that I didn't stay for dinner often enough.

Sam entered through the back door and came through the kitchen to where I sat in the living room.

"Hey Dad, you have trouble leaving on time?" I asked.

"Yeah, old Bernie sent me a bad batch of lumber just before closing. Before I left, I had to call and yell at him before telling him to pick that crap up in the morning. He'll not get a dime from me for that subpar crap!" Sam said as he walked to the liquor cabinet and poured himself a bourbon.

"Well, I hear that's happened a lot with him lately. I wonder what's happening with his company," I said.

"I don't know, but we've been doing business for way too long for him to have sent me a load that looked like that. I don't mind one 2 x 4, or even a couple that are subpar, but not half a batch! That's highway robbery! He said it was his new guy. I told him it had better be, because there was no damn excuse if he's the one who sent that load!" Sam said.

"So, Dad, what did you want to talk to me about? I got the feeling that you are seriously thinking about something." "Well, I've had an offer from a large out of the area company to buy Gentry Construction. I would have never considered that, except that I don't have anyone to pass the business along to since you're not interested. You're still not interested, right? As for your sister, well she'd probably turn around and sell it anyway. So, what do you think?" Sam asked.

"First off, have you asked Mom how she feels about that? Selling the family business would certainly impact her life, as well as yours," I said.

"No, not yet. I'm still up in the air about it all. If I did sell it, we'd be set financially for the future. That alone though isn't a good enough reason to sell what I've put a lot of sweat and elbow grease into for my entire life. On the other hand, maybe it's time. I'm close to retirement age, so I could build a cabin up in Flagstaff and live there easily enough. We'd be out of this damn heat, and right now, being able to fish and hunt whenever I wanted to sounds like a dream existence to me," Sam said.

"Dad, if you and Mom are ready, maybe it's time for a change. Mom could stay here while you're up there overseeing the construction of the cabin," I said.

"Yeah, you know how your mother is about being more than 10 miles away from the reservation. Staying overnight in Flagstaff for a damn powwow is one thing, but I'm almost certain she wouldn't want to live in Flagstaff."

There was an uncomfortable pause, and I suspected that Sam might have envisioned his retirement without Mom since things between them had not been good for a long time. His drinking and their arguments had increased over the years. As for me, I'd gladly do whatever was necessary to help my mother resettle on Nagchaw. Her family, the Yellowbird Clan would be beyond elated to have her away from Sam and living back home again.

As we sat there, Mom and Joslin drove up and parked, and within seconds I heard Jos yelling from outside.

"Keith, get your butt out here and help me carry this stuff inside, please!"

I went outside and although the rain had stopped, the wind was still blowing. I was not surprised to see three large brown grocery bags filled to the brim with I don't know what, but apparently things that Mom desperately needed for our dinner tonight.

As Jos and I carried the groceries in, I came back outside to close the car door. Once I did that, I glanced toward the street and saw a black pickup with a large red stripe down its hood slowly cruising by. The windows were heavily tinted, so I couldn't tell who was behind the wheel or if there was anyone in the passenger seat. Once I stopped to get a better look, the truck sped off. Right then, Jos came out to see what was keeping me.

"Hey, come on in and set the table, please. I've got to help Mom with dinner. You know she thinks she's helping me by letting me do most of the cooking," Jos said, laughing.

"Well, that's good of her. How else are you ever going to find a husband?" I laughed as Jos threw a punch at my shoulder.

"You male chauvinist! I don't need to learn to cook for anyone but myself."

"Okay, okay, just learn to cook so you can feed me when I come over to your place, some-day. Hey Sis, do you know anyone who owns a black and red Chevy pickup? I've seen this one around a couple of times. The windows are heav-ily tinted, so I can never really see who's inside."

"No, but I've heard that this mystery truck has been cruising on Nagchaw lately. Were you aware of that, Keith?" Jos asked.

"Yes, I am aware of that. In fact, it almost ran a few of us down on our way to lunch the other day. Had we not been paying attention, it could have easily struck us as we crossed the street on our way to Naturally Native."

I knew it was my high school nemesis Jack Mitchell. He was looking to get even for my hav-ing knocked him out at The Scarab that night. I had never mentioned what happened that night to anyone but Mike Milton. Mike thanked me and said he'd thought about clobbering Jack a couple of times himself when he'd encountered him around Colemen. I understood what Mike was saying. I felt that way too, but I never would have struck him had he not made those scandalous comments about Telrica. That crossed the line, and I was not sorry about addressing the situation in that manner one bit.

Chapter 15
Looking For Truth

In seeking truth, you have to get both sides of a story.

-- Walter Cronkite, Former News Anchor

After the dinner dishes were done, the four of us sat in the living room, Dad with his bourbon and the rest of us with our glasses of homebrewed iced tea. We talked about anything but what was going on with Dad and the possibility of him selling Gentry Construction. I kept waiting for the subject to be brought up. I even tried to help by talking about Flagstaff and how great the weather was there during the summer. Still, none of that worked. Sam sat in his recliner and glared at me as if he wanted me to stop. And then, I did it. "Mom, do you think you could ever live in Flagstaff?" I asked.

"Oh, no, I don't think so. That would put me about 60 plus miles from our Northern brother's reservation. Whereas Coleman is only about 10 miles as the crow flies from Nagchaw, and that's a reasonable distance, so no I don't think so. Why are you asking Keith? You'd better not be thinking about moving to Flag!" Mom said.

"No Ma, I'm not. I was just thinking about the Thompsons and their relocation from Nagchaw to that area and wondering if you'd ever consider it." I turned to Sam. "What about you, Dad?"

Pausing, Sam glared at me. "Sure, why not. I could hunt and fish any time I wanted. And, if the circumstances were right and I had a decent place to live, why not?"

The conversation continued for a while and moved on to Joslin being able to attend graduate school at Northern Arizona University. As the conversation started to dwindle, Sam started yawning. He got up out of his recliner and said good night and headed off to bed. Joslin decided to get back to her romance novel and went back to her room, which left me and Mom.

"So, son, how is your job going with the Tribal Council?" Marta asked.

"Very well Mom, I'm learning so much. And Jericho Jefferson is the best boss ever."

"Oh, that's good, I'm glad to hear that. He is a good man, so it makes sense that he'd be a good boss too."

"Mom, I know I asked you about him before. It seemed like you didn't want to talk about him or the situation back then. I don't want to pry, but I'd really like to know what happened between you two. And how you ended up with Dad instead of Jericho," I said.

There was a long silence, and Mom got up and took our iced tea glasses into the kitchen for refills. Upon returning she looked at me. "Okay, but you cannot repeat anything I say here to Sam or to Jericho."

"Okay, I promise. I won't say anything."

"It's been many years ago now, but this truth would change everything," Mom said. "Let me start from the beginning, Keith. Grandma Moon arranged for Jericho and me to formally meet at the Tucson powwow that year. I hadn't really dated at all and was very apprehensive about meeting him, except that Grandma said that he was an exceptional man. A man who would become somebody of significance to our people and to me. We had already seen each other around the reservation and he'd said "hello," but I never encouraged him. He was handsome and his energy was strong, which I'll be honest kind of scared me.

"In Tucson, at the powwow, we were formally introduced, and it was obvious he was interested in me from the start. The energy between us was intense, but Keith, I was very inexperienced. I hadn't had any relationships outside of a couple silly crushes which didn't amount to a hill of beans. At that powwow, we spent a lot of time together. He spoke about himself, telling me who he was and what he hoped his future would be. I was very impressed, and yes, completely smitten. He was, and still is important to me, but in a way that I can't really explain, Keith. We were happy together for two years. Two of the best years of my life. I sometimes wonder what my life would be like now, had I not decided what I decided. I think that's all I want to say about it now, son." Marta picked up her glass of iced tea and sipped it slowly.

"Wait, Mom, that's not the end of it. You can't leave me hanging like that."

"Well, that's as much as I can say, for now. Maybe we can talk about this again some other time."

To say I was disappointed that I didn't get more of the story from her is a complete understatement. There was a part of me that just wanted to yell out, *Is Jericho Jefferson my father or not?*" But having promised not to say anything left me wondering if maybe I'd heard enough. What good would it do knowing that my biological father was this outstanding Nagchaw tribal leader if I couldn't acknowledge it to him and everyone else. On the other hand, it would explain why Sam treated me like a stepson all my life. But wait, did Sam even know? By the way Mom spoke, it sounded like he was in the dark as well. What a damn conundrum, I thought. I so desperately wanted to tell Telrica and Pawpaw, but only the latter was good about keeping secrets.

Telrica would be fine with this information for about 5 minutes, then at Naturally Native, or a rehearsal, or talking with her family, she'd spill the details and before long everyone on Nagchaw and in Coleman would know the truth. That, I'm certain, would put an end to the Sam and Marta saga for sure.

The next day at work, I had reason to speak with Jericho privately in his office. After we'd finished our business conversation, I slyly mentioned Mom speaking about their history to me after dinner. That comment had him inviting me to lunch that afternoon.

It was an unusually quiet walk to Naturally Native. We placed our orders with Emmy Jane, and she'd just delivered our iced teas. I could tell Jericho was waiting for me to speak, so I said, "Okay Jericho, Mom made me promise not to say anything to you or Sam. Which means I'm breaking a promise to someone I love more than the sun and the moon. It's important that you know that," I said.

"Oh, look Keith, I don't want to pressure you into saying anything that you're not comfortable with," Jericho said.

"Well, to be honest, she didn't say anything I didn't already know. She basically confirmed what you'd said to me and what I'd heard from her family...Pawpaw to be exact." I paused, then turned back to him. "But I know there's more because when she started, she said something that was very revealing. I don't think she realized that when she said it, but she said, 'It's many years ago now, but this truth would change everything.' The thing is, she never got to that truth. She stopped right at that point and said 'maybe' we'd talk another time, which is a total cop-out," I said.

"Don't be so quick to judge her, Keith. You don't know how that truth might have affected her life."

"That's true, but it's important that she take a risk now because..." I stopped.

"Because why?" Jericho asked.

I sat in silence for what seemed like a couple of minutes before going on.

"Because I want to know if Sam Gentry is my biological father," I said avoiding looking at Jericho.

"Well, Keith, I do too. At the time, I've suspected that your mother got pregnant by me and then married Sam. She was having morning sickness, but she swore to me and probably your Dad, I mean Sam, that she wasn't pregnant. I tried to get her to talk to me about it, but you know your mother. When she doesn't want to talk about something, that's it!" Jericho said.

"Yeah, I know. She's a hard nut to crack," I said as we both laughed.

We finished our lunch and went back to the office. I promised Jericho that if she and I spoke again about their history, I'd let him know. In my heart of hearts, I was beginning to feel that what Jericho said was true. That Mom had been pregnant with me at the time that she married Sam, which means that my biological father is the man I call my boss, Jericho Jefferson.

Chapter 16

As the Eagle Soars

With the wild nature as ally and teacher we see not through two eyes but through the many eyes of intuition. With intuition we are like the starry night, we gaze at the world through a thousand eyes.

Author: Clarissa Pinkola Estes, Ph.D.
from *Women Who Run With the Wolves*

I got back home after dinner and that conversation with Mom, and I was exhausted. I found a note on the kitchen table that Telrica had stopped by and was on her way into Tucson for back- to-back rehearsals. She said she'd be staying overnight with a female cast member, and she'd be back the next afternoon. That was fine with me because all I wanted to do was take a shower and go to bed. While the warm water washed over my body, I heard a distinct voice say...

Truth cannot be hidden. Truth will be revealed.

I'm familiar with these kinds of auditory messages, as I've heard them throughout my lifetime. Mom had me sit down with Pawpaw years ago so he could talk with me about the Yellowbird "gift." Pawpaw shared with me his history with "Spirit messages" and said that our eyes and ears could only see and hear a small fraction of the sight and sound that was going on in the energy world. In other words, there was a whole lot going on around us that can't be seen or heard...except occasionally by those who can receive "Spirit messages."

At any rate, I immediately knew what truth would be revealed. I was happy to hear that, but did Great Spirit know how stubborn my mom was? I had to laugh at that last thought, but honestly, that woman had kept the truth hidden for many years, so what were the chances that she'd come clean now? As I got into bed, I took a deep breath and exhaled. I don't remember anything else after that, as it was lights out.

At about 2:00 am, I heard my name being called. It sounded like Telrica, but didn't she say she was staying overnight in Tucson? I sat up and tried to get my eyes adjusted to the dark. I looked around and saw no one. I turned and swung my legs over the side of the bed and stood up. Feeling a little unsteady on my feet, I moved cautiously down the hallway and then into the living room to the front door. Before opening the door, I peeked out of the living room blinds. I didn't see a thing, so I opened the front door and saw the same: nothing. Closing the front door, I decided to put the safety chain on, and I went back to bed.

Early the next morning, before the sun was up, before anyone in their right mind was awake, I had a brief dream which struck me as odd. In the dream, I walked up to a man who then extended his arms. He motioned for me to hug him, and I did. I tried to see who the man in this dream was but couldn't. All I could clearly tell was that it was NOT Sam Gentry. Upon waking, I had that feeling of certainty that you get when you just know something. My gut was telling me that the man in the dream was none other than Jericho Jefferson.

I stumbled out of bed and walked to the living room blinds and peeked out. The sun was just starting to rise in the East, and I couldn't see outside that well. I removed the safety chain and opened the front door. I stepped out onto the front porch and looked up into the sky. To my amazement, I saw a majestic, brown eagle soaring overhead. As I continued watching, I swear that brown eagle knew he was being observed. Suddenly, this majestic eagle swooped down and soared right over the porch. I watched a large eagle feather float down and land a couple feet away from me. As I picked up the feather, intense energy jolted through my body. It startled me, yes, but intuitively I knew it was an acknowledgement of the things that had been happening over the last day or so.

While the fresh pot of coffee was brewing, I went into the bathroom to wash my face, comb my hair, and brush my teeth before getting dressed for work. As I sat drinking my morning coffee, I pondered the happenings of the last 24 hours and its connection to the brown eagle sighting. The Nagchaw, among other tribes, have always revered eagles. Rising above the mundane, eagles symbolized the ability to observe life from a spiritually enlightened perspective. Eagles represented detachment from simplistic ego desires and symbolized courage, respect, strength, and wisdom. They flew close to Great Spirit. I put the eagle feather on the altar which sat beneath the window in my bedroom.

With the very next thought, hearing my stomach rumble, I decided a breakfast burrito from Naturally Native café would hit the spot. There'd be plenty of time to sit down and eat it there, so out the door I went.

When I arrived, who should I see sitting at a booth, but Jericho. He'd also come in for one of their breakfast burritos. After seeing me, he motioned for me to join him at his booth for breakfast. After placing my order, I turned and walked over to where Jericho was sitting. To my surprise, as I approached Jericho, he got up and moved toward me for a hug. Like a bolt of lightning, that early morning dream sequence shot through me as I experienced déjà vu.

"Good morning, Keith, they make some damn good breakfast burritos here, don't they?" Jericho said.

"Yes, they do," I said, still feeling the energy of the dream and the sudden embodiment of it in Jericho's hug. I looked at him quietly. "Jericho, I have a question for you. So, do you believe that we can receive help from the spirit world as far as being guided into the future?" I asked.

"Whoa, young buck, you're into some heavy thoughts for so early in the morning. What's going on with you, Keith?" Jericho asked

"Well, I've been having some interesting, even fortuitous dreams and auditory messages since my conversation with Mom a couple days ago," I said.

"Look Keith, I'm sure I don't have to tell you that your clan folk have always been revered as intuitive seers. The Yellowbird clan has always had an ability for, or the gift of 'future sight.' That's not to be taken lightly either, because in the hands of an evolved soul, that can be highly beneficial for those connected to that individual."

Yes, I was aware of the Yellowbird "gift" as it was referred to, but I'd heard whispers that Jericho Jefferson had some form of the gift too. I don't know if that was a fact, but the older folks on the Rez hold those who have "gifts of the spirit" in high esteem. And it wouldn't surprise me if Jericho had some form of the Spirit gift too. I've always felt like he and I had some kind of special connection, and maybe that's what it was. One of these days I knew I would get up the nerve to ask him directly about that, but that was going to be one of these days—not today.

As we sat finishing our burritos, one of the elders came up to our table and spoke to Jericho. He spoke in the traditional River People dialect, so I only understood portions of what the two were speaking about. Whatever it was, there was an intensity to their brief conversation, and I'd hoped that Jericho would share the full content with me once the elder left our table.

As the elder turned and walked away, he stopped and looked back at Jericho and then at me before he continued out of the café. I looked at Jericho and waited for him to offer some kind of explanation, but he just continued eating.

"So, that sounded like an interesting conversation," I said.

"Yes, it was. Apparently our people are being gifted with spirit messages of warning, which is a blessing."

"Then that's a real blessing for you, this way you can make sure to keep safe," I said.

"Well, that would be true if the warning message was about me."

Since the conversation with the elder who approached our booth, Jericho had avoided making eye contact with me. I hadn't thought too much about it, as I figured that he was trying to deal with what he'd been told, and how to deal with that.

"So, what, are you saying that the spirit message he told you about was a warning intended for someone else?"

Pausing, and then looking at me with that Jefferson intensity that I'd only witnessed a couple of times but clearly recognized, he came clean.

"Keith, the elder received a warning but it was about you," Jericho said.

"About me? Okay, that's interesting. What exactly did that elder see or hear?" I asked.

"He said he saw you behind the wheel of your truck on the side of the road in a ditch. You'd been in an accident with another truck. A much bigger, newer truck and he saw the truck as it took off after colliding with you," Jericho said.

"So, I'd better pay attention to my driving while traveling the reservation back road then."

"Keith, please, just stay off the back road, it's unpaved and unlit. It's known for having more vehicle accidents. Folks coming back from The 5th Amendment bar at night avoid the main highway. Everyone knows the Tribal PD doesn't patrol that stretch of road as closely," Jericho said.

"That's true. I'll make sure to avoid that stretch, especially at night. That's the last thing I want to have happen right now. Everything in my life is good. I have no complaints, so I'll take heed and listen to the Spirit warning," I said.

Chapter 17
Living Life Forward

Life can only be understood backwards, it must be lived forwards.

– Soren Kierkgaard

As the days turned into weeks and then months, I began having thoughts about how I might handle certain situations or various conversations around tribal policy during our council meetings. It's not that what Jericho was doing was wrong or inferior, but more like my style was different than his. Not by a lot, but enough to be noticeable. I was careful not to push the limits too far while in session with the rest of the council members present. In our conversations afterwards though, I was able to speak more freely with him. I greatly sensed that Jericho liked...no Jericho loved...that I was engaging with him in this manner. This absolutely meant that he was a great mentor, and I was learning a lot from him.

"Hey Keith, do you realize how close we're getting to my retirement? It's just under 4 months away, still I'm beyond pleased with the progress you've made. You're going to be a fine Chief Executive and I'm glad that you've had an unusually long time as my understudy," Jericho said.

"Yes, so am I. Being able to work so closely with you has been the education of a lifetime. Plus, I've come to value your opinion and perspective on almost everything. It's a special bond for me," I said smiling.

"Yes, I feel that deep bond with you too, which I've thought a lot about. It's like you're the son I'd wanted but never got the chance to have," Jericho said blushing slightly.

No sooner than those words left Jericho's lips, Allie the Tribal Council office manager barged into the office. She was somewhat excited and out of breath.

"So sorry to barge in like this, but Jericho, we've got a situation out front that I'll need you to come out and handle. And yes, I've already called Captain Batton," Allie said. "What on earth is going on Allie?" Jericho asked.

"There's this awful man in the lobby asking for 'high school Indian dude,' and he's drunk too. He keeps saying terrible things about whoever it is he's talking about and saying that he wants to file a complaint," Allie said.

I immediately knew that it was my old high school nemesis Jack Mitchell and got up to head to the front lobby, but Jericho stopped me.

"Where are you going Keith? I'll handle this. He's probably had a run in with one of the high school kids and just needs reassuring that we'll take his complaint if he can be civil and calm down."

"No, it's not that simple Jericho. The person he's speaking about is me. There's been bad blood between us since high school. A few weeks ago, after work, I stopped by The Scarab for a quick beer before going home. He was there, drunk, and we had a few words. Everything was fine until he called Telrica a 'hot little bitch,' and I punched him in the face knocking him out. I left the bar before he came to, and he's been on the hunt for me ever since. I've even seen him drive past my folk's place one night when I was there for dinner."

"That might be, but he's here at the Tribal Council office, so I'll handle him. If he insists on being aggressive, Capt. Batton and I have an agreement about these kinds of situations. Batton's always happy to show off Tribal PD's 4-Star accommodations. So, Keith, you stay in my office, he doesn't need to see you here," Jericho said as he winked at Allie. Jericho and Allie walked back to the front office. One of the Tribal Officers, Stanley Kantu, was already in the lobby. Nodding at Office Kantu, Jericho walked up to Jack Mitchell.

"Hello Mr. Mitchell, I'm Jericho Jefferson the Chief Executive Officer of the Nagchaw Tribal Council, how may I help you?"

Looking surprised, Jack stood up and tried to say something before falling back into the chair he'd been sitting in.

"I want to file a complaint about high school dude," Jack said.

"You want to file a complaint about a high school student who lives on the reservation?" Jericho asked.

"Yeah, but he's not a high school kid anymore. That's just what I call him because I can't remember his name," Jack said.

"So, how are you going to file a complaint about this individual if you can't remember his name? And what exactly would your complaint be about?" Jericho asked.

"Oh, there's plenty to file a complaint about. First off, in high school he always thought he was so damn smart. He always enjoyed making me look stupid and that's a big complaint for me. Then, a few weeks ago, I saw him at The Scarab drinking a beer. I spoke to him. Then he got up and punched me in the face. I was out cold for God knows how long. On top of that, the bar owner banned me from ever coming back into his bar," Jack said.

"Well, it sounds like you've had a bad time with this fellow for a while now. First off, I find it hard to believe that you didn't have any part in the situation. And, secondly, if you can't even tell me what his name is, there's no way I can help you file a complaint."

At that point Officer Kantu stepped up and said that he'd escort Jack over to the holding cell until he was sober enough to safely drive himself off the reservation and back to Coleman.

When I got home that evening while waiting to hear from Telrica, I told Mike about the situation at the office with Jack Mitchell. I told him what Jack said and how Jericho handled it.

"Man, Keith, that guy is a real piece of work. I swear that Jack is such a nuisance. You know, I can't believe he's managed to avoid a stretch at the county jail or a longer stay at the state pen," Mike said.

"Yeah, he's a guy that was always looking for trouble in high school. I mean look at how his life has changed since then. In those days he was popular, a star. He had plenty of admirers, and even then, he was so focused on me. For what reason, I never understood. Had he come to me and said he needed help with one of his classes, I would have gladly done so," I said.

"Now Keith, you know that couldn't have happened." Mike said laughing.

"What do you mean?" I asked.

"Come on Keith, you know he couldn't have asked for help with one of his classes. He needed help with all of his classes!" Mike said as we both laughed hysterically.

The phone rang around 6 pm and I answered it. It was Telrica and she asked if we could skip seeing each other that night. She said she was exhausted and just wanted to go to bed early. I said "sure" and told her I understood. That change in plans meant I could go to the house for dinner tonight and check up on Jos and see if Mom was up for another little talk.

As I pulled up in front of the house, Sam was pulling out of the driveway. He was probably going to the bar. He nodded and waved, and I returned the gesture. Once inside the house, the aroma of garlic, green chilies and other spices filled the air. It wasn't a surprise really. I had spoken to Mom on the phone earlier in the day and said I might come by. "Might come by" to my Mom meant you were for sure coming over, so the smell of my favorite crockpot dish with green chilies, garlic, beef, cherry tomatoes, squash, potatoes, and red onions was a favorite. To go along with the Indian stew, her green chile and cheese cornbread topped off one of my favorite meals. Everything but the beef came right out of Mom's backyard planter garden. As I walked to the kitchen table, Jos strolled in with her current book in hand.

"Hey Jos, what's your book about?" I was always interested in hearing about what my sister was reading. The girl's taste went from physics and black holes to romance novels, which I always thought was her quirkiest trait.

"Oh, this one is about an old Shape Shifter that would take on the form of animals leaving him disguised from those around him. Keith, did you know that shape shifting mythology goes back to 13,000 BC?" Jos asked.

"Aww, no Jos, I didn't. You know shape shifting is also a part of the Nagchaw lore. You should ask Pawpaw about that sometime. He's got stories, some real doozies," I said.

"Really? Okay, I'll do that. I want to work on a creative piece about shape shifting to sell at the next powwow. I hope his stories will give me some good ideas," Jos said.

"Okay, come and sit down you two, dinner's ready," Mom chided warmly.

Our lively dinner conversation continued about shape shifting, and we were both surprised that our mother had a couple of stories to tell us. She always seemed so happy when she was speaking about anything related to her family, the Yellowbird clan, and the Nagchaw customs and traditions. She said it was important that Jos and I know the lore too.

After dinner Jos and I cleaned up, while Mom took a cup of her herbal tea into the living room. Once the dishes were done, Jos said good night and went back upstairs with book in hand, we knew she was gone for the rest of the evening. I made myself a cup of tea too and joined Mom in the living room.

"So, Mom, I was hoping that we could continue our conversation from the other night. Our conversation about you and Jericho back in the day."

There were a couple minutes of silence, and I forced myself not to interject any random thoughts. I wanted her to be the one to break the silence. "You know, Son, Jericho and I were so good together. I completely believed that we would get married at some point." Mom said.

"Yeah, that's what Pawpaw and Jericho both said. I just want to understand why you chose Sam over Jericho. It doesn't make any sense to me at all."

"Well, I was young and naïve. Jericho was the first real romantic relationship I'd ever had. When I met Sam, I was attracted to him too. Back then he was charming, and I ended up believing that he and I were meant to be. I know it sounds so ridiculous now, but in a nutshell that's what happened. So, I try to remember that had I not married Sam, we'd have never had Joslin, so she was the gift I got." Mom said.

It took a few seconds before either of us realized what she didn't say. She said "...we'd have never had Joslin..." and not "...we'd have never had you and Joslin..." Stunned at how the truth finally came out, I just sat there and realized that I wasn't completely shocked by that. I looked at Mom and she was teary eyed and looking at me.

"Mom, thank you for being honest. I know how hard it was for you to do that. Honestly, Mom, I'm relieved to know the truth." I paused. "So, does Sam know?"

"I never told him outright. He had questions about the timing of your birth and came to me asking about that. I refused to say either way, and eventually he let the subject go. After you were born, he asked me again, when he saw you for the first time. He said he knew you weren't his son." Mom said with tears streaming down her face. "I guess he never let it go, he's always withheld his love and affection from you. I don't think it was a conscious thing in the beginning, but eventually I know it was. Once he started verbally degrading our people and telling you to stop acting so Indian, I realized this was his way of punishing me. What I did was not right. There was no hiding your appearance, you were Nagchaw through and through. Even a couple of your mannerisms remind me of your father, Jericho," Mom said.

"Well, does Jericho know" I asked.

"I'm not sure, he was suspicious back then about my being pregnant. He asked me, but I outright told him I wasn't pregnant," Mom said. "I don't know what I was thinking. Had I realized that I was carrying you, I know I wouldn't have been able to leave Jericho like I did. Keith, I've paid a heavy price for my mistake. Your father has turned out to be an ill-tempered drinker and you know he's backhanded me a couple of times over the years. I guess I've stayed because I feel I deserved what I got with Sam." Mom finished and began to cry.

"Mom, please, you've paid your dues. There's no reason for you to stay with him. Jos is old enough to take care of herself, and I'm sure she'd go with you back to the Rez. Although Sam is her father, I don't think she respects him much. She's often said to me that she doesn't understand why Sam treats her differently than he treats me."

"We've talked about that. She's always felt like he's been unnecessarily cruel to me."

"Well, he has, Keith. It just angers me to no end. I've tried to get him to be more accepting and compassionate, but his actions speak louder than his words. His actions reveal his resentment and that he's flat out refused to see you as anything other than a 'damn Indian.'"

I stayed for another hour or so trying to comfort Mom. I didn't want to say anything at that point, but shit, I just hit the lotto... My biological father was Jericho Jefferson. My heart was leaping out of my chest. I felt like calling him up and yelling over the phone...Dude, you're my dad!" I wanted to tell Telrica, but I knew she'd gone to bed early, so I'd break the news to her the next day.

I returned home and Mike was still up.

"So, how was dinner? How's the family?" Mike asked. "Mom sent you some of her Indian stew and green chile cornbread." I handed him the Tupperware container. "She said she hopes you enjoy it."

"Man, she gave me enough for a couple of meals. I'll eat some now and take some to work tomorrow for lunch. Please thank her for me. Your mom's a real gem!" Mike said.

"Okay, listen, after dinner we got into a conversation that made my day... It's gonna blow your mind Mike."

"Oh no, what's up Keith. Is she finally gonna leave Sam? You know everyone on the Rez has wanted that to happen for years." Mike said.

"Well, that's my hope too, now that the truth has come out," I said.

"Okay homie, you're killing me with this! What's the scoop Keith?" Mike said.

"Well, I've been pushing her to tell me about how things were back in the day, when she and Jericho were an item."

"Oh, wow, we're going way back there! I've got a feeling I know what you're going to tell me."

"Just listen to me. It's taken some serious moves as Mom's been resistant to talk about her old history. I finally got her to talk about the Jericho-Sam dilemma she faced so many years ago."

"Will you stop beating around the bush. I'm already sure I know what it was you got confirmation on, your paternity, right?" Mike said.

"Shit Mike, I hit the damn lotto. My biological dad is Jericho Jefferson. The most outstanding elder male on the Rez, next to Pawpaw Yellowbird," I said, excited beyond belief.

"Yeah, I always hoped that you'd get confirmation about that someday. Man, I am so happy for you, brother! Now that you two have been working together, it's visually more apparent than ever. It's like looking at Jericho and his younger self. I'm not the only one whose noticed that around the Rez either," Mike said. "When are you planning on telling him?"

"Well, it's tricky given that we're working together. Not to mention as he retires, he'd hoped to be handing the keys to the kingdom, so to speak, over to me. I'll have to think about that for a minute before I go running out and screaming the truth at the top of my lungs down Nagchaw Central. You know that's exactly what I feel like doing, too."

"That's wise, give it some serious thought. I'm sure Jericho will be right behind you shouting the truth down Nagchaw Central too. It's obvious that he's been an admirer of yours from the get- go," Mike confirmed.

We continued talking about my good news for another hour or so and then went to bed. I tossed and turned unable to fall asleep until about 2 am. As I was drifting off, once again, I heard the Spirit message... *Truth cannot be hidden. Truth well be revealed.*

Chapter 18
As Reality Shape Shifts

Not in his goals but in his transitions man is great.

-- Ralph Waldo Emerson

The morning sun rose quickly. My eyes fluttered open, and for a moment I'd forgotten my good news. By the time I was fully awake, I recalled my dinner with Mom and Joslin, and then my conversation with Mike. The next person I wanted to tell was Telrica, so I got up and called her. She was already up, so I told her I was going to jump in the shower. I told her to put on the coffee and I'd see her shortly.

"Good morning sunshine, you're certainly in a chipper mood this morning," Telrica said as I entered her place, and we greeted each other with a hug and a kiss.

"Yes, I am. I have some fantastic news to tell you. Let me get a cup of coffee and join you at the table."

Telrica had a plate of Nagchaw morning buns on the table. These puff pastries were chocked full of savory goodies, not unlike a breakfast burrito, only in a light pastry.

"I had dinner with Mom and Jos last night. Afterwards, Jos went upstairs to read, and Mom and I had a discussion in the living room."

"Where was Sam?" Telrica asked.

"He was leaving as I drove up, and he hadn't returned by the time I left to go home. As you know, I've been trying to get Mom to talk about her history with Jericho before she married Sam. Well, last night I hit the jackpot. I guess she'd started feeling guilty for not being more open with me about who my father really is."

"Oh Keith! Did she tell you the whole story?" Telrica asked.

"Yes, and she went through it all. Keep in mind that this is stuff she hasn't talked about with anyone since before I was born. Anyway, she said that Sam figured out the timing of my birth was off by a couple of months and asked her about it. She told Sam her time of conception was inaccurate, however, as soon as I was born and he saw me, she said he knew I wasn't his son.

"Then Jericho suspected that she was pregnant before she and Sam got married. She believed she wasn't and that's what she told Jericho. Being the honorable guy that he is, he believed her. So, there you go. My biological father is the one person I'd choose to be my father if given a choice, Jericho Jefferson."

"Oh Keith, that's fantastic! I guess you haven't had time to see Jericho about this yet. When do you plan on talking with him?" Telrica asked.

"No, but he's aware that I've been trying to get Mom to come clean about the situation. Believe me, he's anxious to know the truth too. But I suspect that he already knows the truth at some level."

Feeling that I'd be useless at work today, I called in saying that I was taking the day off for some much-needed rest. Yes, Jericho, my father, had pushed the concept of self-care with council employees. He'd stated that we can't expect others to do that if we ourselves can't do the same. Setting a good example is a priority, he's often said.

Saying goodbye to Telrica as she was off to a rehearsal being held closer to home, I told her I had the day off and I'd see her later. As I finished off a second Nagchaw Morning Bun, the phone rang. It was Jericho checking up on me. He said since I've never called in and taken off work, he was a bit worried about me.

"No, I'm fine, thanks for checking. I just got some news that I wanted some time to let settle before coming into work," I said.

"News? Is everyone in your family okay?" Jericho asked. "Yes, everyone's good. I went over to the house for dinner last night. Sam was gone, so after we ate, Mom and I had another conversation about her history. We got down to the truth of it all, all of it Jericho."

The conversation went silent. I knew Jericho understood what I had just said, so I waited for a response. It seemed like he was silent for a long time, but it was probably less than 30 seconds.

"So, you found out the truth about your paternity? And was it good news for you? Jericho asked.

"It was the best damn news of my life!" I paused and then said, "Dad!" as he and I began laughing hysterically over the phone.

"Okay Keith, please know that I feel the same way. Still, let's take a precaution, and verify it beyond anyone's word. Let's go to the health center and do a paternity test. This way, if Sam suddenly changes his mind, he can't claim that what you're saying is a lie."

"Not a problem, I'll do whatever you think is wise, Dad. God, I love saying that!" I kind of yelled into the phone.

"Okay, let me make a phone call to the Medical Director, Doc Watson will want to handle this himself to make sure it's kept completely confidential. I'll call you back shortly." Jericho said.

Within the hour, Jericho called back and said that Doc would be available to meet with us the weekend after next. He said the best time would be on a Saturday, at shift-change, 2:30 pm was when the nursing staff were giving reports between the morning and afternoon shifts. Doc said that we should check in saying that we were there for a meeting with him, and he'd come and get us. He'd do the blood draw in his office so that there was no chance of anyone knowing what was going on. Finally, the truth, and soon the verifiable proof that what Jericho had suspected, would soon be sealed by blood. The reservation lab would have to send the bloodwork out to a lab in Tucson and the results wouldn't be immediate, but still, we'd know before Jericho's retirement party.

In addition, Jericho asked how I'd feel about waiting until his retirement party to make the official announcement. In fact, he wanted a two-fold celebration, his retirement and a father-son reunion party. I agreed that would be fine, because the truth has been covered up for a long time. It was going to take some emotional and mental adjusting for both of us to completely come to terms with that.

Three months wasn't that much time, when you thought about the enormity of what was coming down the pipe. Still, the happiest of the whole lot besides me was Jericho, my dad. We decided not to share our news of the paternity test until we got the official results. Then, the only ones I had planned to tell were Mom,

Joslin, Telrica and Mike. I'd planned to ask that they not say anything to anyone until the two-fold celebration of Jericho's retirement and our father-son reunion party. That gave Mom time to prepare for letting Sam know and I wanted to be with her when she did that.

Then Jericho and I needed to decide how to break this news to the Nagchaw Nation, so there were some things to ponder prior to the upcoming two-fold celebration. It's not that there would be any disgruntled tribal members, in fact, we anticipated that the population for the most part would be almost as happy as we were with the news. It would be the verification of a long-held rumor, by the older generation, about what many felt they've known for years.

Both Jericho and I were carrying on as usual, as far as our working toward my transition into the Chief Executive role and Jericho transitioning out of his long-held lead council position. Allie, Rachel, Jos, and Telrica would be asked to oversee decorating the large first floor meeting room where the two-fold party would be held. The symbolic passing of the torch, aka the two-fold party, was going to be on a Saturday afternoon, but it would have already happened in the office on Friday, the day before.

I often felt like I was in a daze with so much coming to pass. I hoped that Mom wouldn't fret too much about breaking the news to Sam. I'd be there to support her, but still my guess was that she would dread telling him. I couldn't help but feel that Sam might be relieved since it would be official that the "damn Indian" was never his kid. That was never his genetics and that would leave Jos as his only biological offspring.

Chapter 19

The Ancestors Call

Walking, I am listening to a deeper way. Suddenly all my ancestors are behind me. Be still, they say. Watch and listen. You are the result of the love of thousands.

-- Linda Hogan (b. 1947) Native American writer

A cool morning breeze blew as the sun rose in the pale blue sky. The smell of freshly brewed coffee enticed my salivary glands. I woke from a dream that left me feeling full of wonder. I dreamt I was amid the Nagchaw Ancients, and I was being asked about my contributions to the planet. I didn't have to say anything because we were communicating without words. As I looked around, I didn't recognize my surroundings. This place was filled with warmth and comfort, and a feeling that I was home. It was a place that I knew I'd be seeing again at some point.

Jericho Jefferson would be officially retiring in just two weeks. He and I had gone to the reservation health center that Saturday and met with Doc Watson. Doc took our blood samples and sent them off to a lab in Tucson. The results would take 7 to 10 days, depending on how busy the lab was. Even so, the results were expected back before the greatly anticipated two-fold celebration.

Jericho and I were reviewing many of the policies, practices, and official documents in his, or rather my, soon-to-be office. We were having lunch together daily, and I was more than happy with what had transpired with the paternity issue and our relationship. We both were the father and son that we'd always wanted but never had, until now. Once the news was official and the word was out, it would truly be a new beginning for me. This was the happiest I'd felt in as long as I can remember. It felt like my life was coming together and I knew that this was the beginning of a new chapter for me.

Telrica had secured a talent agent, named Michelle Anders. Michelle was having her come out to Hollywood for a couple of movie auditions. They were small parts, but still auditions that would put her on the big screen. She was as excited as ever and she would be back a few days before the celebration. Having gone around and around, she and I had decided that I would move into her place in Coleman. That way I'd be there when she returned home. Apparently, her new agent had anticipated lining her up for more auditions later, and she'd be back and forth between Coleman and Hollywood for a while until she could land a role in one of the big budget movies she was hoping to get.

Jos was waiting to hear about the scholarship she'd applied for and was considering starting the Native American Studies program at the new year. She'd be staying with Mike's cousin, Dora Milton, who would be starting the program with her.

Sam was considering a tentative agreement to sell Coleman Construction at the end of the year. In addition, Sam was talking about building a cabin in Flagstaff. As for Mom, she had made it perfectly clear to Sam that she wouldn't be going to Flagstaff. Not long after that, she and Sam started talking about separating before he sold the business and started looking for property to build his new cabin. With half of the sale of the business, either of them would be able to do just about whatever their hearts desired. Mom's family were expecting that she would finally come home. She would once again be Marta Yellowbird, only now with years of struggles under her belt. Even so, Marta was still the daughter, sister, auntie, and friend that many on Nagchaw had given up hoping would ever return home again.

I found myself thinking that new beginnings were on the horizon for all in the Gentry household as I left work that day. The week had been long, and I was anxious to get home. Telrica had been out of town at an audition and would be back that evening. There was an NFL game on the TV, which I wanted to see from the beginning. The Pittsburg Steelers and the Cleveland Browns game was one I'd been waiting to see all week. I'd be able to make it in time if I cut through the reservation on the back road.

The back road was not paved or lit, but it was only dusk, so it wasn't a treacherous byway at this time of the day. I got into my truck and made my way down Nagchaw Central, and zig zagged through a couple of neighborhoods. I headed down the winding dirt road that ran next to the old ditch until it turned into a long stretch running straight into Coleman. I considere stopping and grabbing a burger and fries 'to go' but decided against that as that might mean missing the kickoff. From the Tribal Council offices, it would take about 20 minutes to get home if I went a little faster than the speed limit. With the window rolled down and the radio on, I started singing along to Bon Jovi's "Livin' On A Prayer" as my hair was blowing in the wind behind me.

Approaching the intersection, I stopped and looked both ways before crossing. There was a pickup truck approaching, but instead of slowing down, this truck accelerated and ran through the stop sign just as I was crossing the intersection. In a split second, that truck collided with my truck, hitting me broadside and hard. The impact sent my truck spinning across the road and headfirst into an old ditch. The driver of the other pickup truck sat on the road momentarily, but no one got out to see who they hit or if anyone was hurt. In fact, the truck engine started and backed up enough to straighten out and then sped off down the dirt road heading into Colemen leaving the scene of the accident.

About thirty minutes later, the Tribal Police got an anonymous phone call about an accident. The anonymous caller said it was on the old back road, about four miles from the Coleman border. The caller also said that he didn't see anyone moving around, so they'd better send an ambulance and he quickly hung up.

Upon hearing about the anonymous call, Captain Batton as he was heading out the door, had Officer's Dakoda and Montera go and check it out with the instructions that if it was anything serious, he should be called at home.

Officer's Dakoda and Montera got into their patrol car and started toward the location of the anonymously reported accident. They both hoped that this call about a truck accident would be a false alarm. As was sometimes the case, they'd find a drunk coming back from the 5th Amendment bar who'd pulled off on the side of the road to sleep it off, or just a couple of kids pranking the Tribal PD. Either way, they'd check it out and call a report back into dispatch once they got there and assessed the scene.

Pulling up to the crash site, the Officer's recognized that there had in fact been a collision that happened, but only one vehicle was at the scene. Before Officer Montera hopped out of the patrol car to investigate, he paused.

"Hey, Dakoda, I know that truck. That's Keith Gentry's truck. Damn, if he's in there, he's hurt. Call dispatch and get an ambulance out here ASAP and a tow truck too. I'll check it inside." Officer Montera said.

Running over to the truck, Officer Montera had to maneuver himself onto its side since it was in the old ditch at an angle. From where he was, he could see me slumped forward over the edge of the seat. Officer Montera got the truck door open and climbed inside. He called out, hoping for a response or movement. He felt the side of my neck, which was still warm, hoping to find a pulse and didn't feel anything. He tried twice more, and still felt nothing. Moving out of the truck, he turned and slowly walked back to the patrol car as Officer Dakoda ran toward him.

"The ambulance is on its way. Is it Keith Gentry? Is he alive? Did you check his pulse?" Officer Dakoda asked.

"No, damn it, man, this is really bad news Dakoda. He didn't make it. It looks like it was a hit and run. I see black and red paint on the impact side, so at least that's something." Officer Montera said.

"Well, let's figure out where the Gentrys live. We'll have to notify them and have someone come out and ID the body. We'd better let Capt.

Batton know about this too. He'll want to notify Jericho Jefferson as soon as the family has ID'd the body. Damn it, Dakoda, I wish this hadn't happened," Officer Montera said.

The two Officers stood in silence for a few minutes pondering the reality of what they were seeing when Officer Dakoda glanced upward.

"Hey Montera, look up. Look at that huge brown eagle flying overhead. I wonder what it's doing out here?" Officer Dakoda asked.

"So, Dakoda, you know the brown eagle lore, right? It's probably escorting Keith's spirit into the Great Beyond. It's considered to be a sign of a Great Warrior when the soul is escorted by a great brown eagle. I'd say that's exactly what's happening as we speak, Dakoda," Officer Montera said as they both continued watching the brown eagle flying overhead in the evening sky.

"Our Nagchaw Warrior has gone to be with our ancestors, The Ancient Ones," Officer Montera said as both he and Officer Dakoda bowed their heads.

The End.

About the Author

Toni was born in San Antonio, Texas on April 20th while her father was stationed at Lackland Air Force Base. Raised as a Roman Catholic, she was the firstborn of eight children, seven girls and a boy. Her bicultural background references her Mexican American father and her mother of European descent. Most of her immediate family lives in Arizona.

She graduated from the undergraduate School of Social Work at Arizona State University and then from the Graduate School of Holistic Studies at John F. Kennedy University in Northern California. Her career has been in the nonprofit Health and Human Services arena, working with multiple underserved populations.

Toni is a twice-published poet and *As the Eagle Soars -- At Birth and Beyond* is the prequel to her first published work of fiction, *As the Twig is Bent -- Between Two Worlds*. She is currently retired and lives in Oakland, California with her long-term softball playing partner, Rick and their cat, Coco. #CatTownRocks